YOU CAN'T KILL A CUPCAKE

THE CUPCAKES IN PARADISE SERIES, BOOK 16

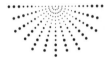

SUMMER PRESCOTT

SUMMER PRESCOTT BOOKS PUBLISHING

CHAPTER ONE

"Welcome back," Fiona McCamish looked up from her desk to greet her boss, neighbor, and reluctant love interest, Coroner and Mortician, Timothy Eckels. "The bodies are stacked high, but I did a bunch of the preliminary stuff so that you can either get into the autopsy or take the simple ones to the mortuary for prep."

Tim pushed his coke-bottle-thick glasses up further on the bridge of his nose and stared at the attractive young woman, entirely unprepared for the news that she'd just given him.

"Was there a train wreck?" he asked dryly.

Calgon, Florida wasn't exactly a booming metropolis. They didn't typically have more than a couple of bodies a week to process in Tim's funeral home, and autopsies were even more rare in the sleepy little beach town. He'd only been gone over a long weekend, to attend an autopsy conference in Vegas, so to come back to a backlog was more than surprising.

"Nope, just a bunch of deaths all at once," Fiona shrugged.

That got his attention.

"Related?" he demanded. "Commonalities?"

"Don't get too excited," Fiona rolled her eyes. "There's no serial killer on the loose in Calgon."

She picked up a stack of folders and flipped through them.

"Car accident, natural causes in a nursing home, natural causes in the hospital, and the only autopsy looks like natural causes, but the police want you to check it out, just to be sure."

"Who's the deceased in the autopsy case?"

"Vagrant. John Doe. I looked him over and didn't see anything suspicious. My bet is that once you get inside, he's not going to have a very healthy liver," Fiona handed him the file.

Tim glanced through it quickly and nodded.

"Okay, we'll start by transporting the three naturals

to the mortuary...I'm assuming they're all going to need viewings and funerals?"

"Two of them for sure. You can make the call on the car accident. The family would like a viewing if possible," Fiona shrugged.

"They'll get one then," Tim stated matter-of-factly.

The man was a genius when it came to reconstructive preparation. He'd made the most mangled accident victims appear as though they were sleeping peacefully. Timothy Eckels had been dedicated to that kind of excellence from the beginning of his career. Body prep was an art form to him, and he was among the best at his craft.

"Somehow I knew you'd say that. Might want to reserve judgment on that until you see the deceased, though," Fiona cautioned, handing him an accident scene photo.

"Oh my," Tim commented, shaking his head.

"Yeah, it'll take a miracle to make an open casket happen."

"No, it'll take skill," he corrected, already going through the steps in his mind. "Let's get those three transported over, then you can meet with families to set up the particulars for the funerals and I'll get started on the autopsy."

"Great, you get to hang out with the dead, and I get to deal with the living," Fiona sighed.

"That's why you're here," Tim commented, heading for cold storage.

He'd hired the spunky young woman to do all of the

things that made him shudder. Her function had initially been to sell funeral packages, make appointments, meet with grieving families – all things that were far out of his extremely introverted comfort zone – and she'd done an amazing job. What he hadn't counted on was the fact that his assistant was smart as a whip and was nearly as fascinated with exploring and processing the dead as he was. The wisecracking sassy lass had been peering over his shoulder and poking her nose into his business for quite a while now, and he begrudgingly had to admit, she had a knack for both finding clues and being his right-hand woman in the mortuary biz. He'd even brought her along when he'd accepted the position of County Coroner. He came with an assistant, they could either take it or leave it. They took it.

Timothy Eckels firmly believed that every corpse had a story to tell, and he'd helped solve more than his share of crimes by paying attention to those stories. His mountain of obscure knowledge about all things death and dying had come in handy more than once, and Fiona was by his side all the way, learning, absorbing, and gazing at her pasty, paunchy boss with admiration that bordered on obsession. She delighted in getting under his skin and he tolerated her impudence because of her talent.

"Gee thanks," she muttered, following him to the storage room to begin transport. "You know, your autopsy will go much faster if you have an extra set of hands," she pointed out, hurrying to keep up.

"And by the time you're done dealing with the logistics of these three, I'll be nearly finished," Tim replied, without bothering to turn around.

"Or, we can get the autopsy knocked out really quickly and then I can go do the human thing," Fiona suggested.

"First, I do not 'quickly knock out' anything, and secondly, we can accomplish more, faster, by working separately," Tim rolled a gurney over to the first storage drawer.

"You're no fun," Fiona groused.

"Never have been," Tim replied honestly, eliciting a giggle from his irrepressible assistant. "You find that funny?" he raised an eyebrow at her, opening the drawer.

"Hilarious," she grinned. "Let's get this dude out."

"You're still here?" Fiona observed, surprised.

She had taken all of the business day to tie up loose ends with the new mortuary clients, and dropped by the morgue, when she realized that she hadn't heard from Tim for hours.

"Clearly," he muttered, deeply engrossed in his study of the vagrant's heart.

"I thought this one was pretty straightforward," Fiona frowned. "Did you find something?"

"Yes, I discovered how important it is not to listen to the suppositions of the untrained," he shot her a look.

"Well, maybe if you took more time to train me, my suppositions would be more accurate," she replied lightly, stepping closer. "Damage," she commented, peering at the heart.

"Correct," Tim said shortly.

"That doesn't look like typical heart disease though," Fiona murmured, trying to get closer.

"Do you suppose I'd still be here if it did?" Tim blinked at her.

"You are a little obsessive, so it's entirely possible," Fiona rolled her eyes.

"I'm not obsessive, I'm thorough. The devil is in the details."

"No, the devil is in the rubber apron. Have you even eaten today, Mr. Cranky Pants?" she demanded.

"I don't recall, and I'm not cranky, I'm focused," he set the heart in a metal pan and pushed his glasses up with the back of his wrist. "You'd do well to follow my example."

"I'm a firm believer that excellence and having a personality don't have to be mutually exclusive," Fiona teased.

He didn't take the bait.

"Fine, I'm here now. How can I help?" she asked, snapping on a pair of gloves.

"Bring me specimen containers for both liquid and tissue. We're going to be sending out multiple samples for analysis," Tim directed.

"You think it's poison?" Fiona's eyes went wide.

"No idea. I've never seen anything like it," her boss admitted, astonishing her.

CHAPTER TWO

Owner of Cupcakes in Paradise, petite, blonde, Melissa Gladstone-Beckett lifted a pan of freshly-baked Gooey Butter cupcakes out of the oven. She'd played with the recipe for a few days and had finally come up with the results she'd been wanting. Her last trial batch had a decadent consistency that was so good, she didn't even really need frosting, but she'd added some anyway, and the results had been spectacular.

"Miss Missy, why ain't you famous?" Beulah, her elderly employee wondered. "You can bake like nobody I've ever seen," she marveled.

"Aside from you, you mean," Missy teased.

"Well now, that just goes without saying," Beulah chuckled, shaking her head.

"Actually, years ago, I had my own baking show, for a very brief period of time," Missy smiled, remembering.

"So, what happened?" Beulah's brows rose.

"She realized that she was forsaking her first love, baking, and quit," a cheery voice from behind them replied.

"Echo, I didn't even hear you come in," Missy grinned, rushing over to hug her flame-haired, free-spirited best friend.

"I'm getting sneaky these days. Motherhood will do that to you," Echo chuckled. "Ohhh...what smells so good?" she went over to peer at the cupcakes.

"Those are Gooey Butter cupcakes," Missy announced.

"Aww...bummer, I wanted one," Echo pouted.

"Never fear, there's a vegan version in the oven. I'll bring you one when I come downtown later today. I have an appointment at one of the city councilman's offices. He's throwing a birthday party for his secretary or something," Missy shrugged.

"Oh, that sounds great," Echo clapped her hands together. "We'll be able to take a cupcake break together."

"Are you working all day today?" Missy asked.

Echo owned a bookstore and adjacent candle shop in a quaint little building downtown.

"Yep, we're having a Winter Wonderland sale, so I'm hoping it'll be pretty busy."

"Oh, that'll be great! I can stock up on new candles and children's books," Missy enthused.

"Me too," Echo nodded. "Did you hear the scandalous news about last night?" she asked.

Missy shook her head.

"I knew Chas got called out on a case in the middle of the night, but I was gone before he came back this morning, so he didn't get a chance to tell me about it."

Detective Chas Beckett was Calgon's only homicide detective, and as such, he was permanently on-call whenever bodies were discovered.

"Let's grab some coffee and cupcakes and take them up front. You can tell me all about it," Missy suggested.

"Twist my arm," Echo grinned.

The two of them met several times a week for coffee and cupcakes before they both started their work-days. Once they were seated across from each other at their favorite bistro table in the eating area, Echo began her tale.

"So, do you remember the neighbor who lives next door to the house that I rented to Fiona McCamish?" she asked.

"Loud Steve? Of course I remember him. He's kind of hard to forget," Missy chuckled. "What did he do now? Is he trying to flirt with Fiona the way he used to with you?"

"Probably, but that's not news. You don't read the paper in the morning, do you?"

"You still get the paper? Welcome to the 21st century, darlin', I get my news from my phone, but no, I didn't have a chance to check anything out this morning. I woke up late," Missy yawned.

"Well, apparently, Loud Steve found a body on his patio last night. When the police got there, he was intoxicated, and the article made it sound like he was a suspect."

"Oh wow," Missy's eyes went wide. "Did you ever get that vibe from him? That he might be dangerous?"

"Dangerous? I don't know," Echo bit into her cupcake, thinking. "He was definitely creepy though."

"Now I'm going to worry about Fiona," Missy sighed.

"I'm sure she's on guard," Echo nodded. "Poor gal has Loud Steve on one side and that weird mortician on the other."

"I think she has the hots for Timothy Eckels, actually," Missy grinned.

"What? Really?" Echo's eyebrows rose at the thought. "What on earth does a gorgeous girl like Fiona see in a guy like Tim Eckels?"

SUMMER PRESCOTT

"Each to their own," Missy shrugged. "I mean...she's a bit...quirky too," she pointed out.

"True," Echo smiled.

When Fiona had first badgered Tim into giving her a job, the mild-mannered mortician had insisted that she submit to a makeover, supervised by Echo and Missy. He didn't want her scaring his clients with her multi-colored hair, piercings and goth-style black makeup. The caterpillar had turned into the butter-fly, and Fiona had owned her new, more subdued look just as brilliantly as she had her rebellious one.

Both women jumped when they heard a muffled shout and a loud thump from the kitchen.

"What was that?" Echo exclaimed as they dashed toward the sound.

"Oh no," Missy whimpered, upon seeing her faithful employee, writhing on the floor, clearly in pain. "Echo, call an ambulance," she ordered, dropping to her knees beside Beulah.

"My heart," the elderly woman gasped.

"It's okay, darlin', we're gonna get you some help," Missy promised, as Echo spoke with the emergency dispatcher.

Her eyes filled with tears, as Beulah gripped her hand, her face tight with pain.

CHAPTER THREE

*F*iona had ordered Chinese food for herself and Tim, while they compiled the autopsy notes on their John Doe, and by the time they finally left the morgue, it was after midnight. Since they'd had to be at two different places during the day, rather than working together, Fiona had driven her own car, rather than carpooling with her boss, as was their usual custom. She hadn't been in her cute rental cottage, which was conveniently located next door to Tim's plain ranch house, for more than ten minutes when she heard a commotion from outside.

Pulling on a light sweatshirt, she ran outside and stood on her front porch to determine where the sound was coming from. Her heart skipped a beat when she saw Loud Steve, her neighbor to the left, pounding on Tim's front door as though his life depended on it.

Everyone in the neighborhood secretly called Steve Stoughton 'Loud Steve' because he had a nasty habit of turning up the music in his little truck so loud that it could be heard long before he entered the neighborhood. To say that he had no friends in the area was a bit of an understatement. In his thirties, he was more than old enough to know better, but a bit too dense to heed the nudgings and subtle suggestions from his neighbors. He despised Timothy Eckels and the fact that he was banging on Tim's door prompted Fiona to action.

"Hey!" she shouted, dashing across the thick-bladed sawgrass in her bare feet. "What's going on?"

Fiona charged across the lawn separating her house from Tim's, just as her boss opened the door. Her protective instincts were on full alert. She didn't like Steve and never had, even when he'd been married to her late sister...maybe particularly then.

"What the heck are you doing here in the middle of the night?" she panted, giving Steve a little shove.

He completely ignored her, swaying unsteadily on his feet, the smell of stale beer seeming to ooze from his pores. He addressed Tim, only slurring slightly.

"Look man, I know you and me ain't never exactly been friends, but I need your help," Steve pleaded, more humble than Fiona had ever seen him, which made her suspicious.

"What could he possibly help you with at this hour?" she demanded.

Tim gave her a mildly offended look.

"Sorry," she mouthed at him, with a shrug.

"I'm afraid I can't help you," Tim said calmly, beginning to shut the door.

Steve grabbed the edge of it, crying out when his fingers were squeezed between the door and doorframe.

"Ow! Geez, hang on! You're gonna say no before you even know what it is? Just listen to me a minute," Steve insisted, shaking his barely bruised fingers. "You're actually the only one who can help. You work with dead people, right?" he asked.

Fiona and Tim exchanged a look, his wary, hers instantly interested.

"Did you kill someone, Steve?" she whispered, eyes round.

"No, but there's a body," he blurted, running a grubby hand through frizzy hair that could definitely stand an encounter with shampoo.

"Where?" Tim's focus was laser-like and immediate.

"On my patio. It's gross, man. I can't even stand to look at it, and there's this weird smell…" Steve began, sounding as though he was trying hard to keep the nausea at bay.

Tim held up a hand to stop the babbling.

"Did you touch it?" he demanded.

"No, I just sorta nudged her with my foot and when

she didn't move, I freaked out and came to get you," he replied, looking faintly greenish in the dim light of Tim's porch lamp.

"Go back to your house and don't touch anything. I'll be over in ten minutes," Tim ordered.

"Ten minutes? Why so long?" Steve complained, one hand on his stomach.

"I have preparations to make and the longer you stand here, asking me questions, the longer it'll take me to get to them," Tim gave him a pointed look.

"Fine, man, geez. I'm going. I don't feel so good anyhow," he grumbled.

"I'll get your bag out of the car," Fiona hurried toward the hearse that Tim parked in his driveway for convenience.

If he got called to pick up a body in the middle of the night, he didn't have to drive all the way to the mortuary to get a car.

"Good. I'm going to place a call to Detective Beckett," Tim nodded curtly and turned to get his cell phone.

Detective Chas Beckett wondered if he'd miss the middle-of-the-night homicide calls whenever he finally retired completely from police work. His mind had been on the possibility lately, since his family business empire in New York needed his help now, more than ever. The senior board member of Beckett Enterprises, who had been installed by Chas' father, and who had run the empire for years, had passed. His loss was felt profoundly by Chas, both on a personal and professional level. The eldest Beckett heir, Chas had balked at becoming a tycoon of industry, preferring instead the simple life of a civil servant, despite his Ivy League education, but now it looked more and more like he might not have a choice.

When the call from Timothy Eckels had come in, he'd chosen to go assess the scene himself, rather than passing it off to a couple of uniforms, fully aware that he might be leaving police work soon. His thoughts lately were consumed by trying to make smart, responsible decisions as to his future and that of his family. Work was a welcome respite.

When he pulled up in front of Steve Stoughton's house, he noticed Steve slumped in a plastic lawn chair on his front porch. Hand on his weapon, he approached slowly.

"Detective Chas Beckett," Chas announced, flashing his badge.

"Yeah, I know who you are," Steve mumbled. "The death guy and the chick from next door are out back, on the patio," he jerked his thumb toward the back of the house.

"I'm going to need to ask you some questions after I assess the situation," Chas warned. "So, you'll need to stay put."

"I ain't going nowhere," Steve sighed, chin to his chest.

"You have any weapons on you?"

"Nope."

"Any weapons in the house?"

"Nah."

"You sure about that, Steve?" the detective persisted.

"Yeah, I'm sure."

"Then you won't mind us coming in to take a look around?"

"It's a mess in there, but you can do what you gotta do," Steve shrugged.

"Why is it a mess?"

"Life, man. Stuff happens. I ain't got time in my busy schedule to be a maid."

Chas nodded.

"Fair enough. Sit tight. I'll be with you shortly."

CHAPTER FOUR

issy sat in the waiting room of the Intensive Care unit, waiting for Joyce Rutledge, Beulah's niece, and Echo's store manager, to arrive. She'd called the vibrant young woman on her way to the hospital as she followed the ambulance in her car. Unable to reach her at first, Missy had left a message, and had given her the scary news about her aged aunt when she finally called back. The poor thing had been horribly distraught, and should be arriving at any moment now.

"Hi, sweetie," she stood and rushed to embrace Joyce when the young woman stepped out of the elevator.

"What did they say?" Joyce asked, her eyes wide with concern.

"I'm not family, darlin', so they couldn't tell me anything, but you should go to the nurses' station to let them know you're here, so they can update you," Missy pointed to the large counter across the room.

"Okay," Joyce nodded quickly. "Are you going to be here for a bit?"

"I'm here as long as you need me, sugar," Missy shooed her away, taking a seat again.

Joyce was taken back into the inner sanctum for what seemed like an eternity. Missy watched seconds tick by on the clock in the waiting area, trying to distract herself with outdated magazines, and failing miserably. One leg bouncing up and down with nervous energy, she kept finding herself staring at pages in the magazine without seeing anything. At long last, a teary-eyed Joyce emerged, looking drained, her face seeming far older than her not quite thirty years.

"How is she?" Missy stood and embraced the young woman, who struggled mightily to maintain her composure.

Joyce uttered a single, tearful laugh.

"She could barely whisper, but she was trying to give me directions to tell you about the baking schedule tomorrow," she shook her head.

"That's our Beulah," Missy smiled fondly. "How's her heart?"

Joyce moved to the vinyl and chrome chairs in the waiting room and slumped into one of them.

"They think that there wasn't a whole lot of damage done. She may have to take medication for a while, but she should be okay," she drew in a shuddering breath.

"Oh, that's great news," Missy breathed a sigh of relief. "Particularly at her age."

Joyce nodded.

"She always has been and always will be a fighter. I love that about her, even when it drives me crazy sometimes," she smiled faintly.

"We all do, darlin'," Missy agreed.

"The doctor says she'll have to take it easy for quite a while, and there are tons of tests that they're going to be doing, so I have no idea when she'll be able to return to work, I'm so sorry," Joyce squeezed Missy's hand.

"Oh honey, that's the last thing that we need to be thinking about right now. You just need to let me know what I can do to help you get our Beulah all healed up and ready to go," Missy assured her. "Her health is the most important thing right now. The rest can be worked out."

"She's going to absolutely hate having to take it easy," Joyce sighed.

"Yes, she is," Missy chuckled. "So, we need to think of creative ways to keep her busy."

"I'm so glad that you were there with her when it happened, and that help came in time..." Joyce trailed off, her throat clogged with tears. "I don't know what I would've done," she shook her head, eyes filling with tears.

"Well, fortunately we don't have to worry about that. We've gotta stay positive and work together to get her better," Missy reminded her.

"I know," Joyce nodded. "Thank you, Miss Missy," she leaned over and gave her a quick hug.

"Anytime, darlin', anytime."

"I hate to have to be the practical one in all of this," Echo sighed. "But what exactly are you going to do without Beulah?" she asked, sipping her coffee as Missy sat across from her, elbows on the table, chin resting on her hands. "You've got events coming up, a major holiday to prepare for, and no help," she pointed out, giving her friend a sympathetic look.

"Girl, I have no earthly idea," Missy sighed. "I mean,

Spencer can help me out in the short term, but he has more important things to do, and I really, really don't like the idea of having to interview applicants to hire someone new. Maybe it's time for me to give up the shop," she mused sadly.

Spencer Bengal was the young, handsome Marine veteran who provided personal security for the Becketts, as well as assisting Chas with his Private Investigation firm.

"What?" Echo's eyes went wide. "You love this place though."

"I do, but I love my babies even more, and if I closed the shop, I could stay at home with them," she shrugged. "I can always bake cupcakes during nap time if I feel the need to be creative," she smiled faintly. "And Kaylee loves to help me in the kitchen, so I can give her tasks that a four-year-old can do."

"Are you ready for full-time motherhood?" Echo asked directly. "I know that when I stayed home after Jasmine was born, I loved it, but when the time came, I was ready to go back to work. Do I sound awful for saying that?" she wondered, her cheeks coloring a bit.

"No, not at all. I totally get it. I'm just...torn. It seems like I don't have enough time to do some of the important things, because I spend a significant amount of time here," she gestured around her, taking in the adorable pink and green décor, cute mismatched tables and chairs, and the expansive glass display case, which housed delectable treats for every palate. "Little Charlie is growing by leaps and bounds, and I feel like I'm missing out on his babyhood. I wasn't there the first time he sat up by himself. Mattie saw it and recorded it on her phone for me, but it wasn't the same."

"What if you cut your hours back? Maybe you could only open up for a few hours a day?" Echo suggested.

"I'd still have to get up before the crack of dawn and do the baking. I'd probably spend more hours baking than I did selling cupcakes if I went about it that way, which doesn't seem very smart from a business standpoint."

"Have you talked to Chas about all of this yet?"

Missy shook her head.

"No. I hate to bother him with anything. He's so busy with helping out the police department, running his own agency, and trying to fill his role at Beckett Enterprises. He doesn't need to stress out over my piddly little situation," she smiled wryly.

"Does it look like you guys are going to have to move to New York?" Echo asked quietly.

"Who knows?" Missy shrugged. "We don't want to,

but it seems like it's getting harder and harder for Chas to be Chairman of the Board while we live here. He needs to be more involved, but he's torn, too. What a mess," she shook her head and picked up her coffee mug, taking a long draw of the life-giving liquid.

"You know that I don't want you to go, but you have to do what's best for your family," Echo sighed.

"Darlin', I just wish I knew what that was."

"I've had to shuffle my schedule a bit too, since Joyce is having to take care of Beulah. It's been challeng-ing, but at least I have Kumar to pick up the slack."

Missy's phone rang just then, interrupting the conversation.

"Oh geez, I have to take this one. It's Councilman Stivers," she gave Echo an apologetic look.

"No worries, I have to get going anyway," Echo gave her a quick hug and waved on her way out.

"Councilman Stivers, how nice to hear from you," Missy lied cheerfully.

She had to hold the phone away from her ear to protect her hearing from the ranting on the other end.

CHAPTER FIVE

"What've we got, Eckels?" Chas asked the coroner, after shaking hands with him and his feisty assistant, who had a habit of calling him Tall, Dark Detective.

"Could be anything," Tim muttered, as Fiona went back to snapping pics of the deceased. "Heart attack, overdose, liver failure. Something just doesn't seem right," he mused, peering at the body through his thick lenses. "When you take a look at the bathroom inside, be careful not to touch anything. I'm going to be taking some samples before your forensics team gets here."

"Samples?" Chas frowned. "What kind of samples?"

Tim thought for a moment.

"Organic matter," he said simply, raising an eyebrow.

"Yeah, it's gross in there," Fiona muttered. "You should have heard the colorful metaphors that Steve-O used when he described it. We thought he was exaggerating, but, unfortunately, he wasn't," she wrinkled her nose.

"Noted. Eckels, do you think there's a possibility of foul play?" Chas asked, taking in the position of the body, the coloring and overall appearance of the deceased.

"I can't pinpoint why just yet, but I'm almost certain of it," Tim nodded, examining the woman's fingernails.

"Okay, I trust your judgment. Let my guys get some photos before you transport," the detective requested.

"Of course," Tim said absently, having moved up to the victim's underarm.

"Might want to use some of that wintergreen petroleum jelly before you go inside," Fiona warned as Chas stepped toward the patio door.

"I'll take it under advisement," he replied, with a perfunctory smile.

He had mixed feelings about becoming involved in this case, and wondered whether he should have delegated it to someone else. He didn't really have the time to get wrapped up in chasing down a homicide. With any luck, it would turn out to be natural causes. Timothy Eckels didn't think so, however, and the quiet coroner's instincts in such matters were generally dead on.

Snapping on a pair of nitrile gloves, Chas stepped inside the cluttered house to take a glance around, before he began questioning Steve Stoughton. He could smell the bathroom before he saw it, and the fleeting thought that he should have heeded Fiona's petroleum jelly suggestion flitted through his mind. Glancing around the tiny befouled room, he made note of a few things, while holding his breath, then made his way back to the front of the house, exiting through the open front door. Steve jumped when Chas stepped out onto the porch.

"Geez man, you can't just sneak up on a guy like that when there's a dead body in the backyard," Steve exclaimed, one hand going to his heart, the other holding a beer.

"How much have you had to drink tonight, Mr.

Stoughton?" Chas asked, shining a pen light in each of Steve's eyes one at a time, to see if his pupils reacted.

"Well, me and Judy finished a case of beer and a handle of rum today, I think," Steve frowned, trying to remember. "And this here," he raised his can of cheap beer, "this is just medicinal. You know, a little something to calm my nerves."

"Are you intoxicated, Mr. Stoughton?"

"No, I ain't drunk. A little buzzed maybe, and seriously grossed out, but I wouldn't say I was drunk," he slurred a bit.

"There's coffee on the way. When it gets here, you're going to drink some of it, and we'll talk more. In the meantime, I'm going to have to ask you to not drink anymore alcohol," Chas warned.

"Oh, I won't. I'm just gonna have beer for now," Steve nodded.

"You are aware that there's alcohol in beer," Chas blinked at him.

"Aww...heck. You tryin' to say that I can't even have my beer? It's just like soda pop for adults, man. I'm the victim here," he groused.

"You're the victim?" the detective's brows rose. "It seems to me that there's a woman lying on your patio who seems to be far more of a victim than you."

"She checked out, she got the easy end of things. I'm the one stuck dealing with all of this."

Chas stared at him for a moment.

"Give me that," he pointed at the beer can in Steve's hand.

"Dude, I'll get you a fresh one. You don't have to drink this one, it's kinda warm," he belched.

"Give it to me now," Chas commanded.

"Wow, you must be really thirsty," Steve frowned. "Keep your shorts on, here ya go," he handed over the beer, almost falling out of his plastic chair when he leaned forward.

Chas took the beer, went to the edge of the porch, and dumped it in the weed-filled mulch of an overgrown garden.

"Hey!" Steve protested weakly. "Not cool, man. Not cool at all."

Chas tossed the empty can onto Steve's lap.

"No more tonight, we clear?" he insisted.

"Crystal," Steve grimaced, folding his arms over his chest.

———

"I really appreciate you helping out with this Spencer," Chas told his head of personal security. "I've got a ton on my plate and I just want to get this solved as quickly as possible if it is actually a homicide," he shoved the manila folder which contained case and evidence notes over to his right-hand man.

"Not a problem. I do have to help Missy out at the shop a bit today, though. I'll take the notes with me and see what I can come up with when we hit slow spots," he took the folder.

"Just don't let any of those pictures sit out where they can be seen, no one will have an appetite for cupcakes if they see that," Chas made a face.

"That bad, huh?"

"I've seen worse, but I'm a homicide detective."

"So, we're proceeding as though it's a homicide then," Spencer confirmed.

"Until we hear otherwise, yes," Chas agreed.

"You got it," the handsome young man began to rise.

"Hang on for a second," Chas stopped him.

Spencer eased back into his seat.

"What's up?"

"As you know, since Chalmers passed, I've been back and forth about whether or not I should return to New York to run Beckett Enterprises," Chas began.

Spencer nodded, his face grave. Chalmers had been like a grandfather to him.

"Would you be open to staying here and keeping the agency open if I left?" his boss asked, looking pained.

"Do you think it will come to that?"

"It's looking more likely," Chas sighed. "I can't trust my family legacy to just anyone, and so far, there haven't been any candidates to replace Chalmers who measure up. Even if it's temporary, I may have to take the reins on a more full-time basis."

"And, since you'll have all of the Beckett resources at your disposal, you could replace me with a team for personal security," Spencer commented, trying to keep his expression neutral.

"I figured you'd prefer to stay here now that you and Mattie are dating," Chas shrugged. "I can turn the agency over to you. You'd have a career for life."

"I was under the impression that I already did," a muscle in the Marine veteran's jaw flexed.

"You are always welcome to be at my side, but I wanted to give you the chance, if you wanted to start a life outside of Beckett Enterprises."

"I've been groomed by Beckett for my entire adult life," Spencer stared at the desktop.

"Just give it some thought. I have a feeling that change is in the wind and we all need to be prepared," Chas said quietly.

"Will do," Spencer's tone was cool. "Anything else?"

"No. We're good for now. My door is always open," Chas held his gaze.

"Good to know."

CHAPTER SIX

*B*eulah Rutledge was a lot of things, but a good patient was not one of them. Joyce was at her wits' end trying to keep the elderly woman calm and resting. She'd asked Missy to sit with the irascible baker for a bit so that she could get some respite by going to work in the bookstore.

"They sent you over to babysit me now?" Beulah challenged, when Joyce showed Missy to her sitting room.

"No, I wanted to see you, silly," Missy grinned, giving her a hug and kissing her papery cheek.

"Mmhmm...and who's minding the store while you're out gallivanting around?" Beulah demanded, pursing her lips.

"Spencer."

"Spencer? That boy is a cute little beefcake, but he can't bake, can he?" Beulah frowned, afraid she'd been replaced.

"I don't know," Missy shrugged. "I think that outstanding young man can probably do anything he puts his mind to, but he's just manning the counter for me at the moment," she reassured her employee.

"You get that order ready for the Councilman?" Beulah peered at Missy over the top of her glasses.

"Oh, that's been such a fiasco," Missy sighed.

"He wasn't in his office when I showed up for our meeting. I knew he wanted to surprise his secretary, so I didn't ask her any questions. I called Mrs. Stivers to talk to her about it, and found out that she didn't know about it either. Councilman Stivers was furious. He called up and chewed my ear off for nearly fifteen minutes."

"Oh lordy, it sounds like you got right in the middle of something," Beulah's brows rose and she chuckled. "Did he cancel the order?"

"He tried to, but his wife insisted that he stand by his order, and made him pay for the whole thing up front," Missy grinned. "I deliver them next week."

"Somebody's in the doghouse," Beulah shook her head.

"I'll still give him some amazing cupcakes," Missy

waggled her eyebrows.

"I need to get back there, Miss Missy," the elderly woman insisted. "You can't be handling all these orders and running the shop too, all by yourself."

"I know, I've been thinking about that..." she began.

"Well thank goodness, somebody's finally talking some sense. I can get off of this couch and get right back to work tomorrow," Beulah sat up straight. "There ain't no need for me to be lounging around, taking a walk once a day and living like some darn old person," her eyes lit up.

"Hold on, honey," Missy raised a hand. "That's not what I've been thinking. So, you know that there's a chance that Chas and I might have to move to New York..." she tried again.

"Oh, say it isn't so, Miss Missy!" Beulah whispered, her eyes sad.

"I don't know yet, but while I've been considering that possibility..."

"You realized you gonna replace me. You can't be waiting around for old Beulah to get better," the elderly woman shook her head. "You got to hire someone else. I get it. I'm telling you though, I'm more than well enough to come back to work. I don't care what them college-educated doctors say. I'm fine. You don't need to hire no one else. I got this."

"Beulah, you need to take it easy and get better, but I'm not considering hiring a replacement for you, I'm considering closing Cupcakes in Paradise."

Missy's eyes filled with tears, just hearing those words spoken aloud.

"Oh no," Beulah's mocha skin paled. "Did I do this to you? With me gone, the work got to be too much?" she whispered, heartbroken.

"Darlin', no! This has nothing to do with you," Missy patted her hand. "If I do close the shop, it'll either be because I'm moving or because I want to be with my babies more. I don't have to work, and I can bake whenever I want," she explained, sad that she'd given Beulah the wrong impression.

Beulah was silent for a moment, taking it all in, but finally nodded.

"I understand," she smiled faintly. "It's gotta be hard being away from those beautiful children every day."

"I feel like I'm missing so much," Missy agreed.

"Well, I'm proud of you, Boss Lady," Beulah patted Missy's knee.

"Of me? Why?"

"Because you figured out what's most important to you. A lotta people spend their whole lives always wondering. You got yourself a fine husband, and two perfect babies, and there ain't nothing wrong with taking the time to enjoy them."

"Thanks, Beulah," Missy swiped a hand under her eyes. "What are you going to do if I close the shop?" she asked.

"Oh, don't you worry none about me," she cackled. "I'll just go work for Miss Echo at that candle shop of hers. Besides, I'm thinking I'm gonna be planning a wedding pretty soon," she grinned triumphantly.

"Really?" Missy's eyes went wide. "You think that Kumar is going to propose to Joyce?" she asked, breathless with excitement.

"The young man called and asked me if he could have supper with me on Saturday night. Now, the way I see it, the only reason a busy young man would want to have supper with an old crone like me, on a Saturday night, is because he's wanting to get my blessing in asking for my niece's hand. I hope that if you do close up shop, you'll still think about making Joyce's wedding cake," Beulah grinned.

"You better believe I will," Missy clapped her hands together. "Make sure you let me know."

"Are you kidding me? I'll be yelling it from the rooftops if my baby girl gets engaged," Beulah chuckled. "It's well past time. I was beginning to think she was gonna be an old maid."

"Thirty isn't old, Beulah," Missy giggled. "But I'm so happy for you, and for Joyce."

"I've been waiting for that girl to give me some babies to love on for a long time."

"Well, let's not get ahead of ourselves. Kumar hasn't even proposed yet," Missy chuckled.

"Better late than never," Beulah shrugged. "I'm not meaning to be inhospitable, Miss Missy, but I believe I'm gonna go lay down for a little bit. Thanks for visiting me. I was hoping you might bring me some of those mint chocolate cupcakes though," she stood and gave Missy a hug, patting her lightly on the back.

"As soon as the doctor okays it, I'll bring you some," Missy promised, as Beulah tottered down the hall toward her bedroom.

"Silly doctors got me eating kale. Can you believe that? Kale. If that nasty stuff don't kill me, nothing will," she muttered, raising a hand in farewell without turning around.

"Sit with me a moment, my love. Let's relish the rare moment when our dearest Jasmine is asleep, and we have a few seconds of quiet." Phillip "Kel" Kellerman took Echo by the hand and led her to the living room for a chat.

"Why do I have the feeling that this is going to be a 'we need to talk' scenario?" Echo trailed along behind her husband, tired after a long day.

"Because you're incredibly perceptive. It's one of the things I love about you," he kissed her hand and led her to the sofa, sitting down next to her.

"Oh boy. Is this about the toothpaste thing? I'll buy

you non-natural toothpaste if you want it, I'm just saying that I wouldn't put all those chemicals in my mouth," Echo shook her head.

"You delight me," Kel chuckled. "And no, I'm more than happy to use your organic toothpaste if that eases your mind. I have something a bit more... monumental to discuss with you."

Echo's heart plunged to her stomach.

"Monumental? Okay, you've got me really worried now, so you'd better start talking," her eyes grew round with concern.

"Relax, beautiful. It's a good thing, not dire news," Kel kissed the tip of her nose. "I have...an opportunity."

"Oh? Well, that sounds exciting. What is it?" Echo breathed a sigh of relief.

"I'm thinking of opening a gallery," he announced carefully.

Echo frowned, confused.

"But you already have a gallery. Do you really think that Calgon is big enough to support two galleries? I mean, maybe during tourist season..."

Kel took her hand.

"I wasn't talking about Calgon, my sweet," his expression was uncharacteristically serious.

"Oh," Echo unconsciously withdrew her hand. "Where were you thinking?" she asked, trying to keep the tremor from her voice.

Calgon had been the only town where she'd felt really at home in her entire adult life.

"There's a partnership forming in Manhattan..." he began.

"Manhattan? That's...interesting. Who would be overseeing it?" she asked tentatively, hoping that Kel wasn't proposing what she thought he might be proposing.

"That's the tricky part," he said quietly. "This is an incredible opportunity that would draw high ticket buyers from all over the globe."

"What are you saying, Kel?" Echo cut to the chase.

"We would want to...we'd need to relocate. At least for most of the year. We could still keep this house for vacations. I'd be bringing in enough revenue that you could come back whenever you like, for visits. What do you think?"

The air was sucked out of the room in an instant. Echo's head swam and she swallowed hard, reeling from the bombshell that her husband had just dropped.

"But...our lives are here," she protested weakly.

"Our lives are wherever we are, sweetest," Kel brush a lock of flame-red hair back from her cheek.

"But Missy's here," she whispered, a single tear sliding down her cheek.

"Somehow I knew that would be your major point of protest," Kel smiled affectionately. "Think about this for a moment...if Missy and Chas move to upstate New York, and we're in Manhattan, where Chas' offices are, you'd only be a train ride away from her. If we stay here and they move, you won't see her nearly as often," he pointed out.

Echo's eyes widened.

"I hadn't thought of that," she murmured.

"Looks like things might just be falling into place for all of us, in a way that we hadn't imagined, doesn't it?" Kel said gently.

"You think so?" Echo whispered.

"We'll see. I'm having lunch with Chas tomorrow. I was guessing that what he and Missy do would have a huge bearing on our decision," he smiled.

"You'd give up the gallery so that I could be here with Missy?" Echo's tears began to flow more freely.

"Well, I'd find a way to make it work somehow," Kel shrugged. "Happy wife, happy life. I know how close you and Missy are. Who am I to break up the dynamic duo?"

"I love you," Echo whispered, moving gratefully into his tender embrace.

"That's what I live for, Dearest," he kissed her hair.

CHAPTER SEVEN

"We were drinking, okay? That ain't a crime, and I can't be held responsible if she drank herself to death," Steve Stoughton insisted, sitting across from Chas in the interrogation room.

"How long before you passed out...?" Chas began.

"Went to sleep," Steve corrected.

"Sure," the detective raised an eyebrow. "How long before you *went to sleep* did the pizza arrive?"

"I dunno...I think I fell asleep with a piece in my hand," Steve shrugged. "Judy started eating, but then started running to the bathroom. I think she just couldn't handle her liquor."

"How much did she have to drink?" Chas asked.

"How should I know? It wasn't like I was watching her. She was acting all stuck up, like she was too good for the likes of me," he looked more pitiful than disgusted.

"Then why was she there?" Chas probed.

"I met her at a bar. She said she'd had a bad last date and wanted to drown her sorrows. I didn't think she meant it so literal."

"Did she say with whom she'd had the bad date?"

"Why would I ask that?" Steve's brow furrowed.

"Which bar?"

"Manley's over on Stalemate Road."

"Nice place," Chas said dryly, his voice dripping with sarcasm.

"Don't knock it 'til you try it. They had three-dollar beers-in-a-bucket and fifty cent wings."

"How long were you at the bar?"

"It's not like I'm looking at my watch all the time. I

don't know. We had to leave when the beer ran out," Steve shrugged, looking uncomfortable.

"When the beer ran out?" Chas repeated, raising an eyebrow.

"Yeah, they sold so many buckets of beer that they ran out. I can't afford that much of the expensive stuff, so we left."

"Was Judy intoxicated when you left the bar?"

"No, not that I know of."

"How did you get back to your house?"

"She rode with me in my truck. We had to stop once on the way home cuz she got carsick. I just turned the radio up so I wouldn't hear it," Steve made a face.

"Why didn't you just take her home at that point? If she wasn't feeling well, why take her to your house?" Chas asked mildly.

"She was fine, just a little carsick. It was her choice. I told her we could go to my house and have some pizza to settle her stomach. It ain't good drinkin' on an empty stomach."

"And you thought pizza would settle her stomach?"

"Usually works for me."

"So, you got home, and your ordered pizza, then what?"

"I got us some more beers and we had a few, then we was eating pizza and I fell asleep."

"Which pizza place delivered?" Chas asked, already knowing the answer.

"Giorgino's. They got a Friday night special."

"And after you fell asleep eating pizza, what happened?"

"I woke up and I had to go to the bathroom, so I went in there and it was bad, so I went to my other bathroom, then I realized that I hadn't seen Judy I thought she might be out back, smoking a cigarette, so I went to look for her out there. I saw her laying there and went to go get the death guy."

"And you'd never met her before that night in the bar?"

"Nope."

"What do you know about Judy?"

"Not much. She didn't like her job much. She was divorced. No kids. That's about it. We like the same kind of music. She thought I was funny and nice. That's what she told me," Steve said, his tone a bit wistful.

"How was she planning to get home after pizza?"

"Her car was at the bar, so I figured that she could either crash at my place, and I'd take her back in the morning, or I could take her back after we had pizza."

"I see. Anything else you'd like to tell me?" Chas asked, a bit frustrated.

He'd deliberately asked the same questions that uniforms had asked at the scene, and Steve's answers were maddeningly the same. So, either he was telling the truth, which seemed fishy at best, or he was a darn good liar. They'd collected a huge amount of potential evidence from his house, which was currently being processed, so Chas would have to interview him yet again, once some actual clues as to what happened were found. Timothy Eckels had sent out multiple samples during the autopsy process, so that was in a holding pattern as well. For now, Steve Stoughton was of no use to him, and he certainly didn't have enough to hold him.

"Alright, Mr. Stoughton," Chas tucked his pen into his jacket pocket and snapped his notebook closed. "I'll want to talk with you again, once we get a handle on things, so don't leave town. You're at the Sleepy Bear Motel for now, right?"

"Yeah. When are your guys gonna be done with my house?" Steve asked.

"Shouldn't be too much longer," Chas stood, leading him to the door.

"Good," Steve lumbered after him. "I'll have to start sleeping in my truck if it takes too long."

"We wouldn't want that. Be sure to give me a call if you think of anything that might be relevant to the investigation," Chas handed him a card.

"Done told you all I know," Steve shrugged and made his way to the exit.

Chas watched him go, feeling like he'd just wasted valuable time.

"Yeah, Roger was doing deliveries that night," Del Parsons, the manager of Giorgino's Pizza told Detective Chas Beckett.

"Is Roger here?"

"Yeah, he's in the back. Lemme go grab him," Del offered.

Chas leaned against the counter, thinking that it had been far too long since he'd had an ooey gooey slice of pepperoni pizza, the lingering aroma of spices in the small shop making his stomach growl. The manager returned promptly, trailed by a thin, glowering young man with pock-marked skin and lank hair that could use a good washing.

"Talk to the man, Rog, and when you're done, you need to finish prepping the delivery boxes for tonight," Del instructed, heading back to the kitchen. "You need me for anything else, Detective, you just let me know," he waved, disappearing into the kitchen.

"I want to talk to you about a delivery you made on Friday," Chas began.

"I made lots of deliveries on Friday. It's our busiest night," Roger mumbled, averting his eyes.

"Do you remember this guy?" the detective produced a photo, holding it out until the young man looked at it.

"Oh, that dude," Roger made a face. "Yeah, I remember him. He wanted to give me a beer as a tip."

"Did he seem to be acting strangely when you were at his house?" Chas asked.

"I mean, trying to give a beer as a tip is a little weird, but he was really drunk," the youth shrugged.

"Did you see anyone else at the house?"

"No, but it sounded like someone was crying in there, and there was a horrible smell. Almost made me sick."

"What did it smell like?"

"An outhouse. What did this guy do?"

Chas ignored the question.

"Anything else you noticed while you were there?"

"Nope. I was outta there quick. I keep my delivery times down, I make more money that way."

"Smart," Chas nodded. "Here's my card. Please give me a call if you remember anything else."

"That dude in trouble?" Roger asked.

"Not that I know of," Chas evaded. "Thanks for your time."

CHAPTER EIGHT

To say that Spencer Bengal had a lot on his mind was an understatement, and he clenched his jaw in frustration when he went to talk to Mattie, the nanny that Missy and Echo shared, and heard sounds of laughter coming from Missy's back patio. Reginald Beckett, Chas' playboy brother, who had just returned from rehab, was a thorn in the Marine veteran's side. Chas was keeping him close, and had asked Spencer to keep an eye on him, so that he would neither relapse and start drinking again, nor meddle in the Beckett family business, at a time when it was in transition. It seemed, to Spencer, that Reggie had taken an uncomfortable interest in Matisse, the nanny, and it set his temper on edge.

"Hey Spence," Mattie waved at him from the pool, where she held on to baby Charlie while the sweet boy sat in an inflatable rubber duckie, and his sister, four-year old-Kaylee, splashed with Echo's daughter Jasmine nearby.

"Welcome to kiddie land," Reggie smirked, perfecting his tan in a lounger next to the pool.

Spencer moved to the side table next to the lounger, picked up Reggie's bottle of water and sniffed it.

"Paranoid much?" Reggie's smile had a dangerous glint to it.

"You have an established track record," Spencer said quietly.

"Do you have time for a swim?" Mattie asked, as Kaylee climbed out of the pool and wrapped herself around Spencer's legs. "Kaylee, honey, you'll get Uncle Spencer all wet," she protested.

"She's fine," Spencer smiled faintly, then picked the adorable tot up for a hug, tickling her and making her giggle. "As hot as it is, I'll dry soon enough."

"You gonna swim with me?" Kaylee asked, patting Spencer's cheek.

"I'd love to, sweetpea, but Uncle Spencer has work to do," he gave her a hug and set her down, his shirt splotched with pool water.

"I don't like work," Kaylee pouted and dashed back to the pool.

"Me neither, princess," Reggie chuckled, stretching and luxuriating in the sun.

"Some of us don't have the option," Spencer gritted out.

"Oh please," Reggie rolled his eyes. "I know that Chalmers hooked you up in his will. Quit playing the impoverished worker routine. Nobody here is impressed."

"Says the man who's never worked a day in his entitled life," the veteran commented, his eyes steely.

"Be nice, boys," Mattie warned, adjusting Charlie's sun hat to protect his delicate button nose from getting burnt.

"I need to speak with you later, Mattie, it's important," Spencer said, turning to go.

"Don't worry, sport, I'll keep an eye on her for you," Reggie taunted.

"I have no doubt," Spencer muttered under his breath, not bothering to acknowledge the comment.

"Spence, are you okay?" he heard Mattie call after him as he reached the patio doors.

He didn't turn around.

"I ordered seven dozen cupcakes from you," Councilman Stivers hissed, while still keeping a pleasant smile on his face, in case anyone witnessed the conversation.

"No, you ordered six," Missy insisted, producing the order form. "Here's the order, and there, down at the bottom is your signature," she pointed.

"Now you know as well as I do that I didn't even read that paper," the smile was getting thinner by the minute.

"I would think that someone in your position would know to always read everything carefully before signing it," Missy shot back.

"I think you called my wife on purpose," the councilman's eyes glittered, making his plastic smile look somehow predatory.

"I think that your guilty conscience is making you a cranky human being, and that is not my problem. If you want more cupcakes, I'm going to have to charge you for more, plus an additional delivery charge and an up-charge for a rush order. Also, if you want to keep arguing with me, I'm going to have to double the rush charge," Missy folded her arms and stared at the councilman.

"You can keep your extra cupcakes, and if I have my way, you'll never work in this town again. Do you have any idea what your meddling has done?" the smile disappeared altogether.

"No, I don't. Should I ask your wife about it?" Missy's kitten-grey eyes turned to steel.

"You're welcome to leave now, Mrs. Beckett," the sour smile was back, and he gestured toward the door. "This is a private function, and I don't believe you have an invitation."

"Have a lovely day, Councilman," Missy replied, turning to go.

"Wow, he said all that?" Echo marveled, as she and Missy sat at the counter in Missy's kitchen, having tea, after the encounter with the councilman.

"Yeah, I was appalled. I don't know how Sharon stays with that man," she shook her head.

"Sounds like you need a glass of wine after all that," Echo observed, raising her tea cup.

"I'd love one, but Chas and I aren't keeping any alcohol in the house while Reggie is here. We don't want to tempt him," Missy sighed.

"Makes sense. How long is he staying?"

"As long as it takes for Chas to figure out what to do about Beckett Enterprises. He doesn't want Reggie going out and making deals, pretending to be in charge, so he's keeping him here," Missy explained. "He seems to be doing really well since he got out of rehab. He spends time with Mattie and the kids and appears to enjoy it."

"Hmm...I wonder how Spencer feels about that," Echo mused.

"Why would Spencer have any feelings about that one way or another?" Missy frowned.

"Well, Reggie is a very attractive man. Seems to run in the Beckett family," Echo grinned and nudged her friend.

"Oh, Mattie wouldn't look twice at Reggie. He's way too old for her, and he's busy trying to get his act together," Missy pooh-poohed the idea.

"You think so?" Echo asked, and inclined her head in the direction of the patio doors.

Missy looked up and saw Mattie and Reggie laughing in the pool with the kids.

"Oh," she blinked, watching the scene outside the doors.

"When's the last time you saw Spencer?" Echo asked.

"When we closed up the shop before my delivery," Missy murmured, staring out the door, seemingly lost in thought.

"And you've been home for a couple of hours now, and there's no sign of him on a beautiful sunny day," Echo pointed out.

"That *is* odd," Missy nodded.

"Might want to talk to him," Echo suggested.

"That poor guy can't catch a break when it comes to his love life," Missy said ruefully.

"If I were half my age and single..." Echo grinned.

"Hey, you watch it, lady, that boy is like a son to me. You don't want to see me go all Mama Bear on you," Missy chuckled.

"Seriously though, Reggie doesn't need to be getting involved with anyone right now, particularly our nanny. He needs to get his life together," Echo frowned.

"That never stopped him before," Missy grimaced. "So, what's new with you?" she asked. "I know you didn't just drop by to have tea," she smiled, knowing her friend all too well.

"Guilty as charged," Echo bit her lower lip. "I'm just bursting with news that I'm not supposed to share just yet, but I can't keep it from you," she confessed.

Missy set her tea cup down and stared at her best friend.

"Well, you certainly have my attention," her brows rose.

"Okay, but you have to pretend that you don't know, because Kel and I were going to tell you after he talks to Chas."

"Oh my, that sounds serious. Are you pregnant again?" her eyes went wide, and she grinned.

"No, thankfully. I think I'm a one kid kinda gal," Echo chuckled. "Kel has an opportunity to open another gallery…" she began.

"Really? I wouldn't think that Calgon was big enough for two galleries," Missy pursed her lips.

"It's not. The new gallery would be in Manhattan," Echo revealed.

"Wow!" Missy exclaimed. "That's wonderful! I'm sure he'd do really well there."

"He would, and his partners would want him to run it," Echo said softly.

"But...how would he do that? When would he have time to create his masterpieces?" Missy was confused.

"We'd have to move there."

Missy stared at her in stunned silence.

"Which means that if you and Chas move to upstate New York, I'd just be a train ride away," Echo reached over and squeezed her friend's hand.

"I definitely need some wine now," Missy said breathlessly, her eyes filling with tears.

"What's wrong? I thought you'd be happy about that," Echo frowned.

"It's just making the possibility of moving seem more real than ever. I love Calgon. It may be slow-paced and a bit political at times, but it's always warm and we have the beach, and my shop, and the dogs love it here," she gestured at Toffee, her loyal golden retriever, who was curled up under her feet, and Bitsy, the spunky little maltipoo who was snuggled into her canine sister's side.

"I'm pretty sure the dogs will love it wherever you are," Echo chuckled. "And besides, Kel said that the new gallery would generate enough revenue that I could come back to Calgon for visits whenever I wanted, and you could come with me."

"What about Mattie?" Missy murmured.

"We won't need a nanny, honey. Neither of us will have to work," Echo pointed out.

"But, she'll need a job."

"We'd give her enough notice and a little bit of a nest egg so that she could find something else, and of course we'd stay in touch, she's family now."

"Why does everything have to change?" Missy wondered, swiping at her eyes. "I loved things the way they were."

"It's the nature of life, Missy. Chalmers passed, and that changed everything. Beulah had a heart attack, and that changed things. Kel has the chance of a life-time, and that changes things. Life happens. We either have to roll with the changes or spend our time fighting them. I know which route I'd rather take, and I think you do too, if you can overcome your fear enough to admit it," Echo's eyes were warm. "The four of us need to go out to dinner and talk about it, once the menfolk have had their power lunch," she grinned. "It's going to be okay. However this all plays out, we have each other," she promised.

CHAPTER NINE

"Ringo chased down the owner of the gun found in Judy Wharton's apartment," Chas told Spencer. "He's on his way down here with the report."

"Great, can't wait," Spencer brooded.

The Marine wasn't a huge fan of the disheveled hacker whom Chas employed to do magical things with his computer, all in the name of private investigating, but he seemed almost surly, and that was more than unusual.

"You alright?" Chas asked, his tone colored with concern.

"Yep," Spencer nodded curtly.

"Hey, Boss Man," a voice drawled from the doorway behind Spencer.

Ringo was wearing grey sweatpants with a mustard stain on the leg, and a flannel shirt that had seen better days. He was in dire need of a shave, and he was chewing on a bite from the hotdog that he held in his right hand, while waving the report in his left.

"Got your report," he announced, tossing it onto the desk and plopping into the chair next to Spencer. "Hey muscle man, how's it going?" he said casually, drumming a hand on the arm of the chair.

Spencer ignored him.

"Interesting," Chas' brows rose.

"What is it?" Spencer asked, leaning forward.

"Gun belongs to the dead chick's boss," Ringo revealed, stuffing the rest of his hotdog in his mouth. "It was a legit purchase. He's got a permit and everything."

"Comments would be better received after you swallow," Spencer remarked, not looking at Ringo.

"Looks like we need to go talk to the boss. Good work, Ringo," Chas nodded.

"De nada, Boss Man," Ringo saluted. "Any chance we can get some Chinese ordered for lunch?" he asked.

"Do you ever go to the gym?" Spencer frowned at him.

"Nah. It's always full of dudes whose biceps are almost as big as their egos," Ringo smirked, heading for the door. "So, about that Chinese…"

"I'll let Holly know to order something," Chas waved him off.

"Good deal. Later all," Ringo waggled his fingers in farewell and left.

"He consumes more in takeout than I make in a month," Spencer grumbled, when Ringo was out of earshot.

"Am I not paying you enough?" Chas asked mildly.

"No. It's fine. Whatever. Where did Judy work?" Spencer stared pointedly at the file folder in front of Chas.

"Green Mill packaging. She was the plant manager's secretary," Chas closed the folder and stood. "Ready?"

"Yep."

———————

"Judy was a good gal. What she did when she wasn't at work was none of my business, but when she was here, she was a hard worker," Red Pfeiffer shrugged.

"When you say, 'what she did when she wasn't at work,' what do you mean, exactly?" Chas probed.

The plant manager's desk was a pile of un-filed paperwork and his trashcan was overflowing.

"Well, let's just say it was no secret that Judy liked to party," he looked uncomfortable.

"She ever party with you?" Spencer asked.

Red's face was suffused with color.

"We had drinks a couple of times. I don't mess around with people at work. It ain't smart," he muttered.

"When was the last time the two of you had drinks?" Chas stepped in.

"Long time ago."

"Weeks? Months? What are we talking about here?" Spencer interjected.

"Months. I don't even remember when," Red's color darkened.

"You two ever go to Manley's?" Chas asked.

"You kidding me? I wouldn't set foot in a place like that. Heard they got closed down a couple of times by the Health Department."

"Do you know if Judy went there?" the detective followed up.

"I'm sure she probably did. She'd go slumming sometimes when she got bored."

"Where were you Friday night?"

"I stayed here until about seven, then I went home."

"Can anybody back that up for you?" Chas demanded.

"My brother Mark was there. He's staying on my couch for a while until he finds work. It's kinda rough having him around all the time, but he's my brother, you know?"

"More than you know," Chas commented dryly.

Spencer shot him a look.

"Do you own a firearm, Mr. Pfeiffer?" Spencer asked.

Red sighed and ran a hand through the wispy

strands of strawberry blond hair that remained on top of his head.

"I figured somebody would get around to asking about that. Yeah, I own a gun. Yeah, I lent it to Judy," he sighed.

"Why did she need a gun?" Chas asked.

"She's a risk-taker, but she's smart. She didn't want to get into a situation that she couldn't get out of."

"Did she carry the gun with her normally?"

"Not that I know of. She said she just wanted to have one at her house, in case anybody followed her home," Red shifted uncomfortably in his chair.

"Was she specifically worried about anybody in particular?" Spencer asked.

"I don't know."

"Why didn't she just purchase a gun of her own?" Chas joined in.

"I don't know. Look, she was just all stressed out about something and asked if she could borrow it for a while, okay? I hate seeing a woman cry, so I gave it to her. That's all I know," Red protested.

"Why was she crying?" Spencer asked.

"I don't know. I think she had some kind of issues with an ex or something," he shrugged, clicking his teeth together.

"What's your brother's name?" Chas readied his pen.

"Mark, but please don't talk to him, it'll freak him out and he's been clean for a while now."

"We're going to need to verify your alibi," Spencer informed him.

"Anything you need to tell us before we talk to him?" Chas asked.

"No," Red refused to look at them, shuffling some papers around on his desk. "We done here?"

Chas stood and stared down at the florid-faced man until Red finally looked up.

"For now," he said simply, then he and Spencer left.

They were nearly to the front door when a soft, feminine voice called out, "Detective?"

Chas and Spencer turned at the same time, seeing a pale, thin, blonde woman hurrying after them.

"Do you have a second?" she whispered, eyes darting furtively about, when she approached them.

"Certainly," Chas exchanged a glance with Spencer and gestured to the door. "Shall we?"

"What's your name, Miss?" Spencer asked, once the automatic doors had shushed shut behind them.

"Marni. Marni Crawford."

The girl trembled a bit and kept glancing nervously about.

"You okay, Marni?" Chas asked.

"Yeah, sure," she nodded too quickly. "I just don't want people to think I'm a rat."

"A rat? About what?" Spencer asked.

"Well, I know you were just in talking to Red, and I'm pretty sure there's something he didn't tell you about Judy," she wrapped her arms around her midsection.

"Oh? What might that be?" Chas asked casually.

"She and Red were...involved," Marni blushed.

"Involved," Spencer repeated. "Like...?"

"Like, she was his girlfriend for a few months and then she got promoted to secretary, even though there were people who were more qualified," she said, with a touch of bitterness.

"People like you?" Spencer asked?

"Yes, and others too. Judy was just a line operator and she moved up real fast."

"How long were they a couple?" Chas broke in.

"A few months," Marni guessed.

"And when did they break up?"

"Months ago."

"But she stayed on as his secretary?" Spencer's brows rose.

"Yep. She started seeing someone else and kept her job too," the bitterness was more pronounced.

"Who was the new boyfriend?" Chas asked.

"I don't know, but rumor was that he was some kind of player," Marni glanced nervously over her shoulder.

"Player?" Spencer asked.

"Yeah, he got around. Not exactly a model boyfriend, you know?"

"Was she still seeing the player when she died?" Chas asked.

"I don't know. She was going out a lot. Went to places I never would have gone."

"Why do you think she did that?" Spencer asked.

"No idea, but I wondered if maybe it was to get back at Red, because he wanted her to act like a lady."

"Did she?" Chas asked.

"Did she what?" Marni blinked, confused.

"Act like a lady," Spencer supplied.

"Oh. I have no idea. She was always real polite and

dressed nice when she was here, but I don't know what she did on her own time. Listen, I gotta go. I just thought that you should know, in case Red didn't tell you."

"I appreciate it Marni. Call me if you think of anything else," Chas directed, handing her a card.

"I will. Don't tell Red where you heard it," she bit her lip before turning to go back into the building.

"Our lips are sealed," Spencer assured her.

The two men walked to the car in silence, but Spencer spoke as soon as they were in Chas' sedan.

"Seems like there's a story there," he observed.

"Agreed," Chas nodded.

CHAPTER TEN

*T*imothy Eckels stared down at Judy Wharton's preliminary lab reports.

"You've been muttering and grumbling over here since those came in," Fiona confronted her boss when she couldn't take it anymore. "What's in those reports?"

"Nothing," Tim frowned, flipping through the file folder for what seemed like the twentieth time.

"You're seriously not going to tell me? How the heck

do you ever expect me to learn if you won't go over the reports with me? You always tell me the cloak and dagger stuff," Fiona bristled.

Tim dropped the file folder on the desk.

"When I said, 'nothing,' I *meant* nothing. The heart has been damaged in a manner that would suggest poison, but there's no sign, as yet, of poison. Everything in the reaction of the blood and tissue points to poison too, but...nothing," he said quietly, his bristly brows furrowed.

"Oh, my bad," Fiona blinked.

"This particular set of circumstances seems familiar somehow, but I don't remember why," Tim said, mostly to himself.

"Well, I can take your mind off of Judy Wharton for a while, but you're not going to like it," Fiona sighed.

"What now?" Tim sighed and took off his glasses, polishing them absently on the tail of his white coat.

"The John Doe that had come in? We need to do a viewing and funeral for him," she informed her boss.

"We don't even know who he is, how are we supposed to have a funeral?" Tim frowned.

"I don't know, but it's paid for," Fiona shrugged.

"By whom?" he stopped polishing.

"No idea. There was an envelope of cash and typed directions in the mailbox this morning. Someone wants him to have a viewing and funeral, and they paid for it with cash."

"Perhaps John Doe isn't a vagrant after all," Tim mused. "Get Detective Beckett on the line for me, please," he directed, lips pursed.

Missy was preoccupied as she went about her routine, taking items from her car into the backdoor of the cupcake shop. Working by herself, with Spencer substituting only every now and then, when he was available, was taking its toll on her, both physically and emotionally. She missed Beulah terribly, but knew that the elderly woman needed time to recover.

She'd been inside for about ten minutes, in the pre-dawn hours, when she heard a noise outside the backdoor. Missy froze, listening, and when she heard the sound again, she hurried to the backdoor, flinging it open.

"Hey!" she yelled, when she saw a lone figure rummaging through her trash cans.

She stepped out onto the back stoop and hurried down the steps as the figure took off running.

"Hey! Stop! Come back here," she called out. "If you need food, you just need to ask."

The person kept running and disappeared behind a stand of palm trees. Missy stood and watched for a while, trying to see if she could catch a glimpse of the fleeing person, but eventually she made her way back inside, her heart thrumming in her chest.

She'd no sooner gotten in the back door than she heard a loud, 'BOOM!' which rattled the windows in their casings.

"Oh lord, what was that?" she whispered, running to the backdoor once more.

She smelled the smoke before she opened the door, and her knees nearly buckled.

"Oh no," she whispered, when she stood on the stoop and saw one of her trash cans on fire.

Running to the hose that was coiled up by the back stoop, she turned the water on and doused the can, which stank of melted plastic. Fearful that the other cans might explode at any minute, she hurried back into the cupcake shop, locked the door and called Chas.

"Well, the good news is, it looks like it was just some kids playing with fireworks," Chas told Missy, holding her tight, while a couple of officers continued to assess the damage.

"Why would someone do that?" Missy sighed against his chest.

"These things just happen sometimes," he kissed the top of her head. "Do you want me to ask Spencer to stay here with you today?"

Missy shook her head.

"No. I know he's busy right now. I'll be fine," she pulled away. "Thanks for coming out. I guess I over-reacted a bit."

"Not at all. Explosions are no joke," Chas reassured her. "You can always close the shop for the day and take it easy if you need to," he rubbed her upper arms, gazing into her eyes.

"No, I'll be fine. Are we still on for dinner with Echo and Kel tonight?" she changed the subject.

"Yep, dinner at the yacht club at seven sharp. If you need some retail therapy, why don't you go buy a new dress after work," he suggested, kissing her forehead tenderly.

"Yeah, maybe I'll do that," she summoned a smile for her amazing husband. "You'd better get going."

"Trying to get rid of me?" Chas teased.

"Yes, I've got work to do and you're distracting me. Now git," she shooed him toward the door.

"Yes ma'am," he grinned, kissing her soundly and heading for the exit.

Missy watched him go, and leaned against the counter for quite a while, staring into space, her mind whirling. Had the explosions been a sign? Was this really the beginning of the end of Cupcakes in

Paradise? She wasn't ready to face that possibility. Not even close. When the last police car pulled out of the parking lot, Missy shook herself and went about her baking. It promised to be a long day and she needed to be ready for it.

Spencer Bengal was waiting for Chas when he got back to the agency. The detective could tell by the look on the young man's face that something had happened.

"What's up?" he asked, settling behind his desk.

"Timothy Eckels called me when he couldn't reach you," Spencer began.

Chas pulled out his phone and saw a missed call.

"Everything okay?"

"Something interesting happened. An anonymous donor paid for a funeral and viewing for the John Doe that he ran an autopsy on," Spencer informed his boss.

"Really?"

"I have the envelope with the typewritten note and the money. It's in an evidence bag."

Chas thought for a moment.

"Good work. Sounds like we have a funeral to go to. Did you inform the Chief about this?"

"Yes sir, he was glad to let us handle it," Spencer nodded.

"Good enough. Anything else?"

"No, sir. Is Mrs. Beckett okay? Do I need to do anything for her?" Spencer softened at the mention of Missy, but had oddly reverted back to formal behavior. *Sir. Mrs. Beckett.*

"She'll be fine. A little shaken up, but you know how independent she is," Chas smiled faintly.

"Yes, sir. I'll take the envelope from Eckels over to the police station once you're done looking at it. Just let me know," Spencer stood and moved toward the door.

"Will do," Chas watched him go, a sinking feeling in his stomach.

CHAPTER ELEVEN

"I'm telling you, I need to speak with Detective Beckett," Steve Stoughton insisted, trying not to raise his voice with the desk sergeant at the police station.

"And I'm telling you, he ain't here," the stout woman behind the counter was stone-faced. "You can either take a seat and wait, or you can leave a message for him to call you. This is the last time I'm gonna tell you. If you stay here and keep badgering me, I'm gonna have to throw you in a holding tank," she threatened.

"I need to see the detective," Steve shouted, just as

Spencer came in the door, carrying the envelope from Timothy Eckels inside a paper bag. "You!" he jabbed a finger in Spencer's direction. "You're the detective's guy. I need to talk to you," he demanded.

"Take it outside and I'll be with you shortly," Spencer towered over him.

"Make it quick though, you're not gonna believe this," Steve muttered, hurrying toward the exit.

Spencer logged in the evidence, making sure it was properly stored, then left the building, hoping that Steve Stoughton would be gone. No such luck. The agitated man was leaning against the building, smoking a cigarette.

"Alright, Stoughton, what is it?" Spencer asked, trying not to let his irritation show.

"You won't believe what I found on my kitchen counter this morning," Steve said in a low voice.

"Roaches?" Spencer guessed.

"Wow, man, that's just rude. This is important," Steve was miffed.

"Alright, Steve, what did you find?"

"Rat poison," he whispered. "Can you believe it?"

"And how do you know that it was rat poison?" Spencer wasn't even mildly interested.

"Because it said so on the box, but that ain't the weird part," Steve moved in closer, violating Spencer's space bubble, but the Marine didn't back down.

"What was the weird part?" he humored him.

"I didn't put it there," Steve announced. "I went to bed and when I woke up, boom, it was there."

"Interesting phrasing," Spencer looked at him more closely, remembering the incident at the cupcake shop.

"Whatever. Do you wanna come see it?" he asked.

"Somebody will come talk to you about it today. Don't touch it and don't touch your doors or doorknobs if you can help it," Spencer directed.

"No problem, man. I'll just hang out on the porch," Steve shrugged.

"Great," Spencer replied, heading to his car.

———

He was being a jerk. As much as it pained Spencer to admit it, he recognized the truth of his assessment. He'd been short-tempered, rude, surly, with everyone and everything lately. There was only one thing he could do to correct that, and he dreaded it. He had to have a heart to heart talk with Mattie and see what she thought about their relationship. His priority in life had been to protect Chas and his family, but now it seemed as though he might be replaced in that capacity. It would be nice to know whether he should stay in Calgon, or follow Chas and Missy to New York, if that's the decision they ended up making. Whether he wanted to admit it or not, Matisse's feelings would play a huge part in his decision.

It had taken him a few days to work up the nerve to have this crucial conversation, and he'd managed to avoid contact with Mattie the whole time, other than an occasional text. But now, he was ready to face his fear and find out what he needed to know, so that he could stop tormenting everyone around him. He pulled into Chas and Missy's circular drive, and grabbed the bouquet of flowers that he'd bought on the way over. The flowers might be a way of saying hello to the beginning of a brand-new life, or they might just be the last token of a final goodbye.

Filled with determination, if not confidence, Spencer mounted the steps and let himself into the comfortable, but elegant home. He figured that Mattie would be upstairs, in the nursery, with Kaylee, Jasmine, and Charlie, but he'd planned his visit around nap time, so that she could slip away to another room to talk with him. If he was really lucky, she'd be out by the pool, baby monitor at her side, reading a book.

Disappointed when he didn't see her through the patio doors, Spencer slipped up the stairs, silent as a ghost, so as not to wake the sleeping babies. When he entered the nursery, he was astonished to see Echo, sitting in the rocking chair, crocheting a sweater for Jasmine. Her face lit up when she saw him, and, placing a finger to her lips so that he didn't speak, she rose and followed him from the room. After a welcoming hug, they made their way to the kitchen, where Spencer finally spoke.

"I didn't expect to see you here today," Spencer smiled faintly, feeling an uneasy mixture of relief and disappointment. He'd psyched himself up to talk to Mattie and finding that she wasn't here was a bit anticlimactic.

"You mean those beautiful flowers aren't for me?" Echo teased, leaning over to breathe in the fragrance of the lovely blossoms.

"Of course they are," Spencer said easily. "Let's get them in some water."

He busied himself with trimming the stems and putting the flowers in a vase with water. Echo watched him, her gaze speculative.

"I'm not blind, you know," she said quietly.

"Excuse me?" Spencer placed the vase of flowers on the breakfast bar and took a seat there.

Echo sat down beside him, her eyes full of concern.

"You're unhappy," she said simply. "My heart hurts for you, sweet boy. What's going on in your world?" she asked, patting his cheek.

"I've got some decisions to make," he replied evasively.

"Join the club, honey," she smiled ruefully. "Is this about Mattie? I'm a good listener, you know."

"I know," Spencer nodded and failed miserably at a return smile. "I don't know what I'm doing," he confessed. "I've turned into this miserable person who doesn't know up from down."

"Oh, you're definitely in good company there. But what's causing you so much stress?" Echo asked, going to the pantry and bringing back a box of cupcakes. She knew that Spencer tended to talk more when food was involved. She put a pot of coffee on, knowing that the cupcake and coffee combination was irresistible to the young veteran.

"Everything. I feel like Chas is just casting me aside, like he doesn't need me anymore. That's probably what hurts the most, but I know he always has a plan, so I'll do what he thinks is best."

The pain in his eyes broke Echo's heart.

"Oh sweetheart, I know that's not the case. Chas and Missy love you like a son. What on earth would make you think otherwise?"

He told her about his conversation with Chas regarding him staying in Calgon and running the private investigation agency.

"Well, I'm sure that's not because he doesn't want you with them, but because he wants you to have your own business. You're great at what you do, but I'd bet my bottom dollar that he offered you the agency because he knows what incredible potential you have. And he realizes that you're pretty smitten with a certain nanny that I know," Echo smiled.

Spencer made a face.

"Yeah, that's the other thing," he admitted. "Where is she anyway?"

A strange look flitted across Echo's features before she could conceal it.

"What?" Spencer's eyes narrowed.

"She's out shopping," Echo hedged.

"Lemme guess...Casanova Beckett is with her," Spencer's jaw tightened.

"Reggie is going through a rough time right now, Spence," Echo said softly.

"Yeah, he is. A rough time entirely of his own making. I'm struggling too, but I take care of myself. Looks like I'll have to continue that," he growled.

"Don't make a snap judgment. We all know that Reggie has his issues, but you need to talk to Mattie, rather than attempting to assign her feelings to her," Echo directed firmly.

"You ever notice that relationships never work out for me?" Spencer asked quietly, taking a huge bite out of a caramel cashew cupcake.

"Believe me, I know how that feels," Echo squeezed his forearm. "I was in my forties before I found the right one. I had given up on being in a relationship, but here I am, happily married, with a daughter and a stepson," she smiled.

"I think the universe is telling me that I should just be alone for the rest of my life," he washed a bite of cupcake down with a giant swig of coffee.

"Nonsense, you're young and have so much love to give. Your whole life is ahead of you, sunshine, you never know what wonderful things are going to happen, but you owe it to yourself to at least talk to Mattie before you write the whole thing off. That's what responsible adults do, and if I know anything, it's that you always do the responsible thing, rather than letting a little bit of insecurity dictate your next move."

"Wow, don't hold back or anything, tell me how you really feel," Spencer sighed, popping the rest of the cupcake into his mouth and reaching for another.

That was definitely a signal that something was amiss. Spencer had a policy of matching his cardio to his carb count, and an indulgence of this magnitude would have him jogging for hours.

"Am I wrong?" Echo challenged, lightly.

Another sigh.

"No. Why do things have to be so complicated?" he muttered.

"Because if things were easy all the time, we wouldn't appreciate them. And because we learn and grow and build character when times are tough."

"I know. It makes me crazy to feel like a victim. I've always been in charge of my own destiny," Spencer finished his coffee and Echo poured him another cup.

"Oh honey, is that what you think?" Echo smiled. "We all try our best to do the right thing, but even the best of us get derailed by life sometimes, no matter how hard we try. You also need to talk to Chas, you know."

"I know. I've been shutting him out. It's not fair."

"Forgive yourself for being human and move on," Echo advised, as Spencer bit into a Coconut Dream cupcake.

"That's harder than it sounds," Spencer's voice was muffled by cake and frosting.

Echo was about to respond, when a soft whimper crackled through the monitor that she'd set on the counter.

"Somebody's up," she said, coming over to give Spencer a big hug. "It's going to be okay, big guy, but you've gotta face things, and give people a chance. Let me know how it goes," she kissed his cheek and headed upstairs.

"Thanks for the talk," he called after her.

"That's what family is for," she smiled at him fondly and headed up the stairs.

CHAPTER TWELVE

"Whoa," Fiona McCamish's eyes grew wide as she stared at the photo. "Timmy!" she yelled, knowing that he could hear her from his office down the hall.

"Stop shouting and don't call me that," she heard faintly.

"Get in here, you have to see this," she commanded.

After what seemed an eternity, she heard Tim's footsteps in the hall, and he appeared at her door.

"What was so important as to prompt that shrill summons?" he sighed, leaning against the doorframe. "You're loud enough to wake the dead."

"That would be interesting, considering our location," she snickered, glancing around the morgue.

"What is it?" Tim pushed his glasses up on the bridge of his nose impatiently.

"Look at this photo," she stood and shoved it in his face.

He snatched it from her hand and examined it.

"Yes, Judy Wharton's heart tissue," he observed. "So?"

"That's just it," Fiona's smile was triumphant. "This isn't Judy's heart, it's our John Doe's heart."

Tim stared at her, then returned his gaze to the photo.

"Get me Detective Beckett," he said softly.

"We're going to test it for fingerprints," Chas assured Steve Stoughton, who seemed to have taken great pleasure in showing the rat poison to the detective. "And we'll test the contents to make sure that it is rat poison."

"I mean, how could it just show up here, right? Somebody had to have broken in, right?" Steve followed Chas like an annoying puppy, constantly nipping at his heels.

"There's no evidence of a break-in."

"Oh, well I may have left the doors unlocked. I do that most of the time," Steve assured him. "Do you think this had to do with what happened to Judy?" he asked, his face grave.

"What would make you say that?" Chas asked carefully.

"I dunno, it just seemed kinda weird," Steve shrugged.

"Did you touch the box at all?" Chas asked.

"Nope. No sir, I just left it where it was," Steve insisted.

"Okay. I'll follow up with you later then," the detective headed for the door, escaping before Steve could delay him any longer.

Chas had two more rather unpleasant stops to make before dinner with Missy, Echo and Kel, and he wanted to get them out of the way as soon as possible.

"We're a bit overdressed under the circumstances, don't you think?" Spencer asked Chas, taking in their expensively tailored suits.

Both men dressed well, unless they needed to blend in during an investigation.

"Maybe," Chas shrugged, preoccupied. "We got a name on the John Doe. Melvin Kemper."

"Does that tell us anything?"

"Not really. He's not local. Came from the East Coast, but hasn't lived there for years. Hard to track, but looks like he's been homeless his entire adult life, and drifted to Calgon four years ago. He was only thirty-four."

"Thirty-four?" Spencer was astonished. "I would've put him in his fifties at least."

"Street life can age a man," Chas commented.

"So, does anything in his background point to why he might have been murdered?"

"Nope, but I got a call from Eckels about him. Said his autopsy was similar to Judy Wharton's."

"Oh great. So, we may be dealing with a serial killer," Spencer sighed.

"Too early to tell, but yeah, and we have nearly no

leads. Lab results aren't conclusive in either case, and we haven't had a match on any of the partial fingerprints from either scene."

"Well, hopefully Melvin's mysterious benefactor will show up to the viewing today."

"We can hope."

"So, we're going to Manley's after this?" Spencer confirmed.

"Yep."

"I'm going to change first."

"Good call," Chas nodded.

There were no cars in the parking lot at the mortuary when Chas and Spencer arrived. That wasn't exactly a surprise. No one expected a huge turnout for the viewing of a possibly murdered homeless guy. Fiona, dressed in a smart rose-colored suit, greeted them enthusiastically.

"Wow, I love it when a double dose of handsome walks in the door," she grinned, hands on hips.

"Good morning, Miss McCamish," Chas greeted her with a smile, while Spencer chuckled. "Any visitors yet?"

"Believe it or not, there is someone in there," she whispered. "He came in right after we opened the doors."

Chas and Spencer exchanged a glance.

"He's alone?" Chas asked.

"Yep. He walked by the casket to look at Mr. Kemper, and he's been sitting in one of the pews ever since."

"Thanks," Spencer gave her a brief smile as they moved toward the small chapel inside the mortuary, their footsteps absorbed by the plush velvet carpet.

It looked as though Chas and Spencer were merely paying their respects when they filed slowly past the casket, but in truth they were looking for anything that might be out of place. Serial killers sometimes attended the services of their victims in order to leave clues with the dead, or to take final souvenirs. Both men watched the lone figure in the pew with their peripheral vision, making certain that he didn't disappear while they were preoccupied with the body.

Timothy Eckels had done an impeccable preparation job, as usual. The body that had been presented to him had borne all the hallmarks of a man who'd lived on the streets. Poor dental hygiene, an almost permanent layer of grime, and lines of perpetual worry and strife etched on his face had all been expertly erased and Melvin Kemper, in repose, had been transformed into a regular stiff, who merely looked a bit older than his thirty-four years.

After their covert inspection of the body, a look passed between Chas and Spencer and with a slight nod to indicate their agreement, they approached the lone mourner in the pew. Spencer blocked any chance of exit on one side, and Chas slid into the pew on the other.

"Friend of yours?" Spencer asked, noting that the clearly homeless man's eyes had grown wide with suspicion and fright.

"Yeah. What's it to ya?"

The man's words were mushy, the result of significant tooth loss. Chas flashed his Calgon PD badge and the guy instinctively backed away. He tried to push past Spencer, who moved subtly to the left, effectively blocking his escape.

"You hungry?" Chas asked mildly.

The man blinked and swallowed.

"I could eat," he scratched at his ear nervously.

"Want me to stay here for the rest of the viewing?" Spencer asked Chas.

Chas nodded.

"Do periodic checks outside too. There may be an observer that we need to know about. When they close him up," Chas nodded at the casket, "join us at the diner."

"Will do," Spencer nodded.

"You, come with me," Chas directed, speaking to the homeless man, who looked like he might just cry.

"I ain't done nothing," the man muttered, but followed Chas obediently out of the pew.

Something had fallen out of the man's pocket as he trailed after Chas, and Spencer waited until they were out of the chapel before he snapped on a nitrile glove and picked it up. Wrapping the small object in the glove, he pocketed it and headed for the door to do a perimeter check.

Betty, the iron-haired and iron-willed owner of

Betty's diner, raised an eyebrow at Chas when he entered her establishment, followed by a homeless man. It was only the detective's loyalty and generous tipping practices that made her refrain from commenting. She nodded to a booth in a dark corner and Chas nodded back, recognizing the instruction.

"What'll ya have, Detective?" she came over with coffee, her order pad at the ready. "You watching your waistline or are you actually going to eat today. No kale specials around here, honey," she smirked.

"I'll take the lunch special, Betty. Thanks," Chas didn't bother with a menu.

"Think you can handle it, Slim?" Betty teased.

"I'll try my best."

"And you?" she turned to Chas' lunch companion.

"The same, please," the man spoke quietly, causing both Betty and Chas to stare.

Once Betty had bustled back to the kitchen to place their order, Chas observed the man across from him speculatively.

"What's your name?"

"What difference does it make?" the man asked, with none of the backward accent that he'd affected in the funeral home.

"Depends. How hungry are you?" Chas asked mildly.

"You'd deny me food to make me talk?" the man challenged.

"I'll do what I need to in order to get to the bottom of a homicide case, and right now, your behavior is making you look like a possible suspect," the detective drilled him with a glance.

"Oh please, you and I both know that I'm not a suspect, and until you started interrogating me, I had no idea that homicide was even a possibility with Melvin," the man rolled his eyes.

"Name, or we continue this pleasant conversation down at the station."

"Nathan Ramsdale. Happy? Can I eat now? Please, Mr. Detective, Sir?" Nathan's voice oozed contempt.

Chas texted the name to Ringo for more information.

"I find it interesting that an Ivy League educated man has been living on the streets of Calgon," Chas observed. "What's your story, Nathan?"

Nathan stared at him, nonplussed, saying nothing.

"You're wondering how I knew. My name is Chas Beckett," the detective explained, waiting for a reaction.

Recognition flickered in Nathan's eyes.

"I recognize your accent and inflection. Your bearing and the way you seated yourself are a dead giveaway too," Chas continued. "Harvard men are easy to spot, if you know what to look for."

"Why on earth is the heir to the Beckett throne wasting his time with human refuse in Calgon, Florida?" Nathan countered. "I'll wager that your story is far more interesting than mine."

"I'm not implicated in a homicide," Chas said simply.

"I got caught up in an insider trading deal because of my brother-in-law. Disgraced the family, lost my inheritance. Couldn't face anyone so I moved south. Ended up on the streets and stayed there. Happy?" Nathan glared.

"Not in the least. Seems a waste of a good education. At any rate, what can you tell me about Melvin?"

"Not much. He was a poor kid from Boston who moved south to get warm," Nathan shrugged. "His tent was next to mine under the same bridge."

"Any idea who might want to kill him?" Chas asked, drawing a curious look from Betty as she set down their food.

"Nah, he was a nice guy. There was the guy in the car though," Nathan mused, unfolding his paper napkin and setting it, rather primly, in his lap.

Good breeding never changed.

"Guy in the car?" Chas repeated, squirting a blob of catsup onto his plate, next to a heaping mound of fries.

"Yeah, some guy came and picked him up a couple of times. I minded my own business and didn't ask what it was about," Nathan cut his burger in two and picked up half for a bite.

"What kind of car?"

"Black, late model Caddy. Nice ride," Nathan covered his mouth with his hand so that he could speak while chewing with what few teeth he had left.

"I don't suppose you happened to notice the license plate number?" Chas asked hopefully, salting his fries.

"I did actually, but I don't remember it," Nathan chased his bite with a swig of coffee. "It was a vanity plate. Made me wonder why somebody with that kind of money was hanging out with Melvin."

"But you don't remember what it said?"

"Nope," Nathan took another bite.

"Did you ever see the guy?"

"No, I tried not to look too closely," Nathan chewed thoughtfully. "Having too much information can be dangerous in my world," he sighed. "Ignorance is bliss, unfortunately."

"Then how do you know it was a guy?" Chas challenged.

"Lucky guess," Nathan glared, putting two fries into his mouth at once.

"When's the last time you saw Melvin with the guy?" the detective let it go.

"A day or two before he died, maybe."

"How was his behavior before he died?"

"He didn't leave his tent much. Said he was sick. There was an awful smell coming out of that tent. I packed up my stuff and moved to the other side of the bridge. Next day, you guys came to pick up the body."

"Who called the police?" Chas asked, noting that the call had been logged as anonymous.

"No idea. I don't have a phone. I don't think anybody else under the bridge does either."

Chas and Nathan ate in silence for a few minutes.

"Who paid for the funeral, Nathan?"

"No idea. That one surprised me," Nathan shrugged.

"We're having the instructions and the money tested for fingerprints."

"Seems like a smart idea. A little shortsighted maybe," the homeless man commented, licking a smear of catsup from his finger.

"How so?" Chas asked, surprised.

"Oh, come on, Beckett, you're smarter than that. Anybody who has the means to pay for a funeral in cash isn't likely to have his or her fingerprints registered in your database," Nathan rolled his rather rheumy eyes.

"Maybe we'll get lucky," Chas remarked lightly, frustrated by his response.

Either Nathan was one cool cucumber who could lie

quite skillfully, or, he was telling the truth, which put Chas exactly nowhere.

"Maybe," Nathan pushed his empty plate away. "Kinda sad that the only ones who showed up for Melvin's viewing were me and you. He was a nice guy. I hope that if someone did kill him, that you find them and make them pay for it. No matter what echelon of society produced them," he said with more than a touch of bitterness.

"That's the goal," Chas wiped his mouth and finished the last of his coffee. "Pie to go?" he asked.

"No thanks, I'm watching my weight."

"Last stop before dinner," Chas commented, pulling into a parking space at Manley's bar. The object that Nathan dropped had been a matchbook from

Manley's that was identical to the one that was found in Judy's apartment.

He and Spencer had changed into casual clothes and would still stand out like a sore thumb among the regular clientele.

"Hopefully you'll still have an appetite," Spencer made a face.

"I'd like you to join us, if you're free," Chas invited. "It's me, Missy, Echo and Kel. We're going to be discussing some rather important decisions, and as a member of the family, I'd really like to have you there."

Spencer nodded once, then looked away, unable to speak past the lump in his throat. He and Chas got out of the car and headed into Manley's. The place was dimly lit, even in the daytime, and smelled of stale beer and broken dreams. The bartender was a paunchy guy with a bad haircut, who looked up from polishing glasses when they came in.

"I've paid my taxes, and haven't committed any crimes, so how can I help you, gentlemen?" he grinned.

"Ever see this gal?" Spencer asked, showing him a photo of Judy Wharton.

"Sure, she comes in every now and again," he nodded.

"Ever see her with this guy?" he showed a photo of Steve Stoughton.

"Yep, Steve's a regular. I kicked the two of 'em outta here the other night. Quit serving them, cuz they looked like they'd had enough, and the woman just about destroyed my bathroom."

"Vandalism?" Spencer asked.

"Uh, no. I think she had a little too much to drink and had quite the accident. I had to hire a guy to clean it up," he grimaced.

"How do you know it was her?" Chas asked.

"We don't get many chicks in here. She was the only one it could've been."

"Ever see her with anybody else?"

"Sure, she's had a couple of guys who seemed like they were her boyfriends. She'd come in here with them sometimes," he shrugged.

"What kind of guys?" Spencer asked.

"Normal dudes, it was kind of strange, really. She seemed like a nice gal. Why would she bring her dates here? We ain't exactly the Ritz," he chuckled.

"Ever see her with this guy?" Spencer pulled out yet another photo, this one of Red Pfeiffer, Judy's former boss.

"Yeah, but it's been months. She was coming in here with a different guy the last few weeks."

"Do you know who he was?" Chas asked.

"No, but he acted like he was some kinda hotshot. I wondered if she was using Steve to make him jealous."

"Did you happen to see what kind of car the hotshot drove?" Chas had a hunch.

"Shiny black car. Caddy maybe," the bartender shrugged again.

"You see the plates?"

"Nope, didn't look that close. Just surprised me to see that kind of vehicle in our parking lot."

"You ever let homeless guys in here?" Spencer asked.

"Hard to tell. A lot of the joes that come in here don't look as neat and tidy as you two," the bartender smirked. "They got money, they can drink. I only kick 'em out if they've had too many or if they smell up the place too much."

CHAPTER THIRTEEN

"What a great table, Chas. I'm going to let you make all of my dinner reservations from now on," Echo teased, taking in the ocean view.

The five of them, Missy, Chas, Echo, Kel and Spencer, were seated in a private alcove at the seafood restaurant on the water. The floor beneath them was thick glass, and they could see waves lapping at the shore below them. Their location in the restaurant afforded them privacy and the most magnificent views in the area.

"And the food is just as amazing as the view," Missy smiled.

Spencer sat, quietly listening to the banter going back and forth around him, sipping at his wine. He was keeping an eye on his phone, because he just had a feeling that there might be a break in the Judy Wharton case soon. Throughout the meal, he nodded and smiled when it seemed appropriate, all the while wondering what the topic of discussion might be, when they finally got around to it. Once coffee and dessert arrived, Missy finally broached the subject that had them collectively on the edges of their seats.

"I'm so glad that we could get together like this," she began, her eyes moist as she looked at the dear faces around the table. "Y'all are my family, and I can't begin to tell you how much you mean to me," she began, then took a breath.

Chas reached for her hand and she clung to the warmth of his as though her life depended upon it. Kel spooned chocolate mousse into his mouth as though his life depended upon it, and Spencer sipped frequently at his wine, but aside from that, everyone was still, giving her their full attention.

"Chas has thought long and hard about what to do with his leadership role in his dad's company, and it's been getting more and more difficult for the poor guy to sit in board meetings online, manage his private investigation agency, and be the lone homicide consultant for the police department. He's been running himself ragged, even with your expert help, Spence," Missy nodded at the young man, who gave her an uneasy smile. "Something has to give. I've been going back and forth about what to do with the cupcake shop, especially now that Beulah is out of commission for a while, and may never come back to work, depending on her heart. So, Chas and I have just been out of sorts and stressed and confused for quite a while now," she smiled ruefully.

"Entirely understandable, dear lady," Kel

commented, dabbing at his lips with a napkin.

"Join the club," Spencer sighed, eliciting smiles from the others.

"So, have you made any decisions?" Echo asked, clutching at Kel's hand under the table.

"Actually, we have," Missy nodded.

"Well, don't keep us in suspense," her best friend prodded with a soft laugh.

"We've come to a compromise, of sorts," Missy announced. "I'm going to keep the shop open, sort of..." she began.

"How does one sort of operate a shop?" Kel teased.

"Well, if she'll do it, I'm going to ask Mattie to take over running it, at least for most of the year, because Chas and I are relocating to New York," Missy looked at her husband for support and he kissed her hand.

"Permanently?" Echo asked quietly.

"Not yet. We're going to keep the house here for now, too. I'm envisioning spending winters here. That way I can still work in my shop when I want to, but most of the rest of the year will be spent in New York," Missy let out a breath.

"Well then, that settles it. Kel will be opening a gallery in Manhattan, and we'll do the same thing," Echo grinned. "It'll be a new adventure."

"Congratulations," Spencer said softly, raising his glass and trying his best to smile.

They all toasted, and Chas turned to the quiet young man beside him.

"Spence, you're a part of our family and always will be. You've protected me, even when I had no idea that you were doing so. You've literally put your life on the line for me, and I can never make that up to you. You'll always be my first choice for personal security. The job is yours for the rest of your life, if you want it," he promised, swallowing hard. "You're like a son to me though, and if you want to break out on your own and run the investigation agency, it's yours. You decide, and Missy and I will support you a hundred and ten percent, no matter which choice you make. We just want you to be happy."

Chas held out his hand, and when Spencer shook it, he pulled the young man in for a fierce hug. There wasn't a dry eye around the table when they separated.

"The worst part of all of this lately, was when you

shut me out, Spence. I can't live with that. Whatever you do, you've gotta talk to me," Chas said, his voice hoarse.

Spencer nodded, his throat working, unable to speak.

"I think a toast is in order," Kel commented, waving to the sommelier, who brought over a magnum of champagne.

Glasses were filled, eyes were wiped, and Kel spoke.

"To new adventures, loving families and smooth transitions," he toasted.

In the clink of crystal and the voicing of 'cheers,' no one noticed that Spencer was even more quiet than he'd been before the announcement, his upcoming decisions weighing heavily on him. Chas' text tone went off and he frowned when he looked at it.

"Everything okay?" Missy asked, seeing her husband's expression.

"New development in the case. Spence, can we take your car to the station?" he asked.

"Of course," the young man nodded, action being his comfort zone.

"We have to go, love," Chas leaned over and kissed Missy tenderly.

"Do what you need to, and be careful," she squeezed his bicep and smiled.

Echo watched the two men leave, a strange look on her face.

"What is it, darlin?'" Missy asked.

"A new beginning for us seems like a new ending for Spencer. One that he didn't expect," Echo murmured.

"I'll talk to him," Missy promised.

———

"What have we got?" Spencer asked, once he and Chas were on their way to the police station.

"Nathan Ramsdale is there, insisting that he speak with me."

"Did they say about what?"

185

"Nope, apparently he's refusing to say anything to the guys on duty," Chas sighed.

"Maybe this will be our big break," Spencer shrugged.

"Here's hoping. Let's stop by the diner on the way in."

"Think he'll hang out and wait that long?"

"I told the guys to detain him for loitering if he tried to leave," Chas smiled ruefully. "He'll appreciate the delay when he sees the food, and it'll loosen his tongue a bit, I have a feeling."

"Smart," Spencer nodded.

CHAPTER FOURTEEN

"I thought I'd see daylight again before you showed up," Nathan complained, arms crossed.

"And I thought you might appreciate a bit of sustenance for our conversation," Chas shot back, plonking the heavy white paper bag of food down in front of him. "Betty's special tonight is fish and chips. Enjoy."

Nathan's attitude magically changed, and he dug into the bag with gusto.

"What've you got for us?" Chas asked, watching the educated homeless man devour his food as though it might be his last meal.

Nathan chewed, swallowed, and took a long drink of the iced tea that had come with the meal.

"I remembered the name," he said, stuffing a handful of fries in his mouth.

Chas wondered if the 'starving homeless guy' behavior was for Spencer's benefit. He suspected that Nathan was smart enough to be able to wangle regular meals, though perhaps not as tasty or substantial as this one.

"The name of what?" Spencer asked.

Nathan looked at the young man, but directed his answer to Chas.

"The name on the vanity plate. It was GO GITR68. I saw it drive by today, and I remembered to take a look."

"How do you know that it was the same guy who used to pick up Melvin?" Chas asked, astonished at how quickly the food was disappearing into Nathan's gullet.

"Custom rims. They have little red lines on them."

"Good work, thank you," Chas said, as Spencer texted the info to Ringo, who texted back within minutes.

"We got a name," Spencer announced, looking at his phone. "And you're not going to believe this."

Nathan finished his food and was sent on his way, after declining an offer of a candy bar from the vending machine. Chas stared at Spencer when the younger man told him to whom the vanity plates belonged.

"Okay, but that still doesn't establish how, and we need to find a way to match the fingerprints, since they aren't in the system," the detective pointed out.

Chas' text tone sounded again, and he looked at his phone.

"This just may be our lucky night," he told Spencer. "Timothy Eckels has a theory. Says it's...unusual."

"Theories usually are when they involve Eckels, but he's almost never wrong," Spencer observed. "If you want to go talk to him, I'll work on getting some matching prints first thing in the morning."

"How do you plan to do that?" Chas asked.

"Just by being a good citizen," Spencer smiled.

"Sounds good. We'll regroup in the morning then."

"Perfect."

Spencer Bengal came out of City Hall the next morning, satisfied with a job well done. His mood changed, however, when he received a text from Chas.

"Oh, you've got to be kidding me," he read the article that the detective had sent, and plugged an address into his phone for directions. "I'm definitely going to change clothes before this," he sighed.

Councilman Brent Stivers glanced up from his desk when the door to his office opened.

"Detective Beckett, and my latest campaign contributor, Spencer," he greeted them effusively, standing up, shaking hands, and gesturing to the seats in front of the desk. "To what do I owe the pleasure, gentlemen?"

"We were in the neighborhood," Chas smiled, taking a seat.

"Good of you to drop by," Brent nodded.

"I'm thinking of going out of town," Chas began.

"The detective needs a vacation," Spencer added, nodding.

"Oh?" the councilman gave them a confused smile.

"Yeah, I'm thinking maybe...India. You've been there recently, haven't you, Brent?" Chas asked pleasantly.

His smile melted away and he paled slightly.

"Uh, why...yes, yes I have. Interesting country," he nodded, fidgeting with his pen.

"Interesting indeed," Spencer agreed. "You know what I find fascinating? They have this tree there, in India, called the Cerbera Odollam. Have you heard of it?"

The rest of the color drained from the councilman's face and he dropped his hands into his lap, not quite in time to hide the shaking from Chas and Spencer.

"Er...no, I can't...can't say that I have heard of that particular tree," he stammered, a thin sheen of sweat beading on his upper lip. "If you gentlemen will excuse me, it's been a long day, and I'm not feeling well..."

"Oh, this won't take long," Chas assured him.

"Yeah," Spencer continued. "They call it the suicide tree because the fruit of it is so poisonous. It leads to a pretty gruesome death, but what's really crazy is that it's virtually undetectable...unless you know what you're looking for," he leveled his gaze at the now-squirming councilman.

"Are you familiar with Timothy Eckels, Brent?" Chas broke in.

"I...ummm...no, not, not personally," as he loosened his tie.

"Well, he's our County Coroner, and he just got back from a conference in Vegas. You know what he learned out there?" Chas asked.

Brent shook his head numbly, looking as though he might just pass out.

"He learned how to detect poisons like the one from the Cerbera Odollam tree. Go figure, last week, he didn't have that information, this week he does. Funny how fate works sometimes, isn't it?" Spencer took over. "And then...here's a coincidence that I'm sure you'll appreciate, Brent. I went over to your house this morning and poked around in your trash a little bit. Guess what I found, in there, among all of the ice cream sandwich wrappers? As luck would have it, Brent, I found a cut up piece of fruit from that very Indian tree. Imagine that."

Brent Stivers dropped his head to his desk and wept.

"Here's the other funny thing, Councilman," Spencer continued, loudly enough so that he could be heard over the crying. "When I was here making my campaign contribution to you this morning, right before I went through your trash at home, you threw a paper cup in your wastebasket right over there," he pointed. "I collected that paper cup when you left to get me a receipt, and lo and behold, the fingerprints on it matched the fingerprints collected at both murder scenes, and on the box of rat poison that you left at Steve's, hoping to throw us off. It's a little insulting that you thought we'd fall for that, Brent, I gotta tell ya."

"Melvin was just practice for you, wasn't he, Mr. Stivers?" Chas asked rhetorically. "Judy was the main target, poor lady. Her biggest mistake was getting involved with you, and threatening to tell your wife about it. Yeah, we found her emails and texts to you, once we knew where to look. Also, were you aware that even dive bars have security cameras? There's footage of you and Judy coming in there quite a few times. Even that one time where you slipped something into her meatloaf sandwich. So, we've got an eyewitness who saw you pick up Melvin, right before he died, and his life counts just as much as Judy Wharton's, so you're going down for his murder too, then there's the footage from Manley's and all of the other evidence we've got for Judy. There are two officers outside right now who are going to take you into custody. What do you have to say for yourself?"

Brent Stivers raised his head, tears and snot streaming down his face, and bawled.

"I want my lawyer."

CHAPTER FIFTEEN

*R*eggie Beckett staggered out onto the back patio, where Mattie was reading her book, while the kids napped peacefully upstairs.

"Hey beautiful," he slurred, clearly intoxicated.

"Oh no," Mattie muttered, feeling a mixture of pity and dismay.

She and Reggie had become friends, of sorts, and it hurt her to think that he had relapsed.

"I think I'm gonna go for a swim," he proclaimed, peeling off his shirt and stripping down to his boxer shorts.

"Oh no, you're not," Mattie yelled, jumping from her lounger.

Reggie started to sway, and she rushed to his side, keeping him upright, and attempting to walk him to the cabana to sleep it off.

"Hey," he mumbled. "You're hot."

The fumes on his breath smelled foul, as he moved in for a kiss, and she flinched, but not in time. His mouth came down on hers, hard, and she struggled to push him away, one arm around his waist so that he wouldn't fall and hurt himself. The experience nearly made her gag, and she knew that she'd have to tell Chas about it as soon as possible. She couldn't be around him, and the children definitely shouldn't see him, if he was going to behave in this manner. She was so intent upon helping the dangerously drunk man, that she never saw that she was being watched.

Spencer was so relieved. His experience helping Chas solve the murders of Judy Wharton and Melvin Kemper had solidified his decision. As tough as it would be to be away from the Becketts, at least for a while, he was going to stay and run the investigation agency, hoping to take Chas' place as a homicide consultant with Calgon PD, as well.

Now, all he had to do was talk with Mattie about the decision. She'd been his primary reason for wanting to stay, aside from enjoying the investigative work, and he had to make sure that she felt the same way he did. He'd picked up another bouquet of flowers and made sure that he arrived at Missy's house right at nap time.

When he pulled into the circular drive, he was frustrated to see Reggie's bicycle tossed carelessly on the front porch, but he was determined that if he encountered Chas' brother, he'd simply tell him that he needed a private moment with Mattie, and leave it at that.

His heart speeding up with the excitement of having made a decision and wanting to share the good news with Mattie, he came in the house and headed for the nursery. Creeping up the stairs, he found all three children sleeping peacefully, and happened to glance out the window. What he saw made him stop dead in his tracks. Moving to the window, he looked down and saw Mattie approaching a barely clothed Reginald Beckett. She wrapped her arm around his waist and tilted her face up to speak to him. Reggie lowered his head, kissing her soundly, and Spencer couldn't watch another second.

In that instant, his plans changed. He wouldn't be able to stand being in a town that had so many memories of Mattie in it. His stomach churning, he tossed the bouquet in the nursery trash can and bolted down the stairs, out the door and away from Mattie. Forever.

A NOTE FROM SUMMER

Dear Readers,

If you're faithful followers of the Cupcakes in Paradise series, you may be worried that this is the end of that series. You are correct, it is, but don't stop reading now, lol. Just as the Frosted Love series evolved into the INNcredibly Sweet series, which evolved into Cupcakes in Paradise, another evolution is happening which I'm hoping you're going to absolutely love!

I'm starting a new series called The Calgon Chronicles, which will bring you stories of your favorite characters from the previous three series. So, you'll be able to keep up with what's happening with Missy and Chas, Echo and Kel, Tim and Fiona, Spencer, Janssen and the rest of the gang. Some of them will be in different locations, but their adventures in sleuthing will go on.

I sincerely hope that you've enjoyed Missy's time in Calgon as much as I have, and it is my dearest wish that you join us on our continuing journey, no matter where she may roam. I couldn't do what I do, without all of you, and I'm forever grateful that you let me share my stories with you.

Love and hugs,

Summer

ALSO BY SUMMER PRESCOTT

Book 2: Coconut Creme Killer

Book 3: Caramel Creme Killer

Book 4: Chai Cupcake Killer

Book 5: Streusel Creme Killer

Book 6: Peaches and Creme

Book 7: Marshmallow Creme Killer

Book 8: Boston Creme Killer

Book 9: Bourbon Creme Killer

Book 10: Spiced Latte Killer

Book 11: Toffee Apple Killer

Book 13: Peppermint Mocha Killer

Book 14: Sweetheart Killer

Book 15: Killer Me Green

Book 16: Blue Suede Killer

Cupcakes in Paradise Series

Book 1: Vanilla Bean Killer

Book 2: Star Spangled Killer

Book 3: Salted Caramel Killer

Book 6: Home Grown Murder

Book 7: Bittersweet Murder

Box Sets

Cozy Mystery Sampler

Standalone Novels

A Match Made in Murder

Christmas Reunion Killer

Home for the Holidays

Thrillers

The Quiet Type

AUTHOR'S NOTE

I'd love to hear your thoughts on my books, the storylines, and anything else that you'd like to comment on—reader feedback is very important to me. My contact information, along with some other helpful links, is listed below. If you'd like to be on my list of "folks to contact" with updates, release and sales notifications, etc.... just shoot me an email and let me know. Thanks for reading!

Also...

... if you're looking for more great reads, I am proud to announce that Summer Prescott Books publishes several popular series by Cozy authors Gretchen Allen and Patti Benning, as well as Carolyn Q. Hunter, Blair Merrin, Susie Gayle and more!

CONTACT SUMMER PRESCOTT BOOKS PUBLISHING

Twitter: @summerprescott1

Blog and Book Catalog: http://summerprescottbooks.com

Email: summer.prescott.cozies@gmail.com

And...look up The Summer Prescott Fan Page and Summer Prescott Publishing Page on Facebook – let's be friends!

To download a free book, and sign up for our fun and exciting newsletter, which will give you opportunities to win prizes and swag, enter contests, and be the first to know about New Releases, click here: http://summerprescottbooks.com

Made in the USA
Columbia, SC
07 June 2021

39334914R00131